THE FLIGHT OF THE
SCHIMMERPLOTZ

ALIAS BRAINS AND BRAWN
BOOK ONE

CHARLES A. SALTER

δ
Dingbat Publishing
Humble, Texas

THE FLIGHT OF THE SCHIMMERPLOTZ
Copyright © 2020 Charles A. Salter
Primary Print ISBN 979-85-86045812

Published by Dingbat Publishing
Humble, Texas

TABLE OF CONTENTS

DEDICATION

This book is dedicated to Gunnar Grey, owner, editor, and chief dingbat of Dingbat Publishing. Having read and published my first work with these two fictional characters, Brex and Jacks—the short story "The Herndon Secret" in the anthology *Death Do Us Part*—she encouraged me to write the first book of a possible series starring them. This book is it, and I thank her for supporting, editing, and publishing this volume.

1

First Contact

Until the incident which changed me forever, when a window into an infernal alternative reality opened in the sky, capturing my secret agent partner and young daughter, we three were having a grand time in Battery Park in lower Manhattan. It was a lovely sunny Saturday in early autumn, with maple leaves turning red and gold. The sky above glowed blue with happiness and the promise of a dry, crisp day, with only fleeting, fleecy clouds high up revealing the cool winds which soon would descend on New York City in the coming weeks.

I paused beside the Korean War Veterans Memorial, a fifteen-foot-tall granite stele with a soldier framed in silhouette, while Brex, my partner in a new top secret government agency, darted ahead with my six-year-old daughter Sara, his god-daughter.

Brex or Brexxie, AKA Breslin Herndon, was reputedly the smartest man in the world, with the intellectual powers of Einstein, Oppenheimer, James Bond's fictional Q, and half a dozen real Nobel Prize winners all rolled into one. The United States would be much less secure without the spy satellites, advanced commo gear, electronic devices, field agent protective devices, and super-secret weapons springing from his fertile grey matter.

But he was a tiny fellow, not much larger than my little Sara. To see them walking together from behind, you would think he was Sara's older brother at most. Only when seeing his face or noting his adult clothes—always the scarlet Gants shirt and grey chinos he loved to wear—could one tell the age disparity.

She was still just in elementary school. He and I had known each other literally for a lifetime, both of us born and raised in Covington, Louisiana, at the height of the so-called Cold War and after it was won.

Now Sara laughed and listened intently as Brex pointed out the various plants, their proper species names, and the peculiar properties of each. At that moment, he was looking at a common foxglove plant, its numerous purple bell-shaped blossoms dangling off the long upright stem. "Sara, that's a *Digitalis purpurea* plant. It's very poisonous if you just randomly eat any part of it, yet it naturally produces a medicine we know as digitalis, which can save people's lives if they have certain kinds of heart problems."

"What's a heart problem, Uncle Brexxie? You mean like a broken heart from being in love?"

"No, angel, that's a different kind of heart, a metaphorical one. I mean this organ in your chest which pumps blood throughout your entire body." He pointed at his own chest.

She placed her hand over her own heart. "I can feel the heartbeat, Uncle Brexxie. I pledge allegiance to—"

Suddenly I saw them both staring into some kind of void. I don't know how it happened, or even what happened, but there was something suddenly hanging in the sky in front of them.

I looked up and made out a vague shimmering, like a mirage in the desert, but with a defined border. A large window in the sky which suddenly appeared, displaying something within which had caught their attention.

I was 25 or 30 yards behind them and could not see into the window, but I tried to angle around behind it and see what lay on the other side.

There was no other side. Behind it I saw only the same trees, bushes, and sidewalk as before, only from a different angle. I watched in astonishment as both of them appeared to be standing there, just staring into empty space— mesmerized, totally engrossed in what they saw through it and on the other side.

Then a strange but loud and angry voice emanated from the void. "Ur dicto bhaggrot."

At least that was the way my ears perceived it. I had no idea what the voice actually said, but my brain picked up the signals from my ears and tried to translate them into English lettering. I also had no idea what it meant, if anything. For all I knew, it held no more significance than a dog's bark, a walrus' grunt, or a clap of thunder.

I heard Brex answer back, "Nidrasan per geblin! Nid!"

Then Sara screamed.

Brex shouted, "Run, Sara! Run to your daddy! I'll stop this guy."

I bolted to the front side of the window and saw humanoid hands, dirty and covered in coarse hair, emerging from it and grabbing Brex around the neck in a chokehold.

Crying, Sara flew towards me and leapt into my arms.

I cradled her tightly and snuggled her close. "It's okay, Sara, I've got you. You're okay."

I could see at an angle now into the window, but only partially. I saw a fierce, angry face leering at Brex. The figure was dressed in some kind of uniform-like clothing, brown with black highlights and ornate insignia suggesting high rank.

Brex could not break the chokehold directly, but he grasped the sides of the window and rapidly closed it onto the strange arms until they released their hold and retreated within to some kind of dark space. Like slamming a door on an intruder trying to sneak into one's house after one had wisely left the chain lock secure on the door.

Somehow Brex sealed the void and, with a wave of his hand, tossed the rapidly shrinking and now bullet-sized globule into the air, where it quickly dematerialized into the blue nothingness of the open sky.

By the time I reached him, still holding my sobbing, precious girl tight, Brex looked weak and wobbly. Barely standing upright, he began to quiver and started to fall backwards to the pavement. I reached out one hand and steadied him.

He squatted on the pavement and took deep breaths, his grey eyes betraying terrible fear. Some kind of existential threat had just crossed our paths, but I couldn't guess what it was. I knew only that my best friend in the world and my only child were terrified beyond all measure.

"What was that, Brexxie?"

"I can't tell you. Your primitive primate brain could never comprehend it."

I sat on a nearby bench in the park and pried Sara's tight hands from my neck, setting her on my lap and rocking back and forth. Then with my right hand I gently stroked her head, flowing with lustrous brown hair woven into an elegant pony tail on the back. "What was it, sweetie? What happened? What did you see?"

"Dad, it was horrible!" She still quivered in my arms.

"What, sweetie?"

"Some kind of monstrous creature was ordering all these other beings around, forcing them to build some kind of tunnel. I snuck into the tunnel and tried to see what was inside. There was a kind of train thing down there. Kinda like a subway underground. I crept closer, trying to see what they were loading into the train, but the bad boss guy saw me and yelled some weird words."

"Wait a second, sweetie. All I could see was you just standing there on the park sidewalk."

"Maybe just my body. But somehow I was on the inside, running for my life through all kinds of weird buildings while all the bad guys were chasing us."

"Us?"

"Uncle Brexxie helped me. He led me to a tower with an open window, took my hand, and we both jumped through, back to here. Then he wrestled with the bad boss while I ran to you. It was awful, Dad! But Uncle Brexxie saved me."

I looked over at Brex with a new sense of admiration and gratitude.

He smiled wanly, still trying to catch his breath, still looking as frail and weak as a Louisiana pussy-willow in a Gulf hurricane.

I cleared my throat. "What was the weird language I just now heard you and that bad guy talking?"

"Oh, that. You know I can speak fluently nineteen current human languages. And I can read at least the basics in fifty-one others. I still haven't mastered Urdu, though. That's a tough one."

"Brexxie, I'm grateful, more than you can ever know, for saving Sara. But don't push your luck. I want some answers and I want them now. I've never seen nor even heard of anything remotely like this, but you seem to know all about it, and you'd better tell me. Right now. PDQ."

"But, dear Jacks, what is the point of me trying to explain something you can never understand? Your brain just isn't that advanced! Just stick with what Sara told you already. She already expressed in the only way you'll be able to understand what just happened to the two of us."

I growled softly. My papa bear instinct was rising and about to overwhelm my sworn duty to protect him. I had previously retired from my job of protecting Breslin Herndon when he used to work for DARPA, the Defense Advanced Research Projects Agency. But then, when he quit that job but the government convinced him to do special projects on a freelance, as-needed basis, I was hired back to protect him once again. Now I worked for a new agency that was so secret, most of the operatives in the monogrammed agencies (such as the FBI, NSA, and CIA) had never even heard of it. The recently formed Space Agency had a newly created top secret group known as the Cosmic Intelligence Group—CIG—and I was their most senior hire.

Little Sara rocked on my lap. "Come on, Uncle Brexxie. What do you call that weird language?"

"Oh, that was Origanis."

I tried to restrain my temper. "I never heard of that, Brex. I may not be able to speak and read as many dozens of languages as you, but I've at least heard of most of them. And I never heard of Origanis."

"That's probably because it hasn't been spoken on Earth for about eight thousand years now. Naw, let's say roughly seven thousand, nine hundred fifty, plus or minus seven point eight."

"What?"

"It's the original tongue of humanity. Back in the Middle Paleolithic period. You know, before the Tower of Babel. The language all the early humans spoke before they decided to build a ziggurat into the heavens and become like gods. You remember how the real God didn't like that and destroyed their tower and gave them a thousand different

tongues so they wouldn't be able to coordinate such diabol-
ical efforts ever again?"

"Of course I do. But if it has been gone from Earth for
that long, then who taught it to you?"

"No one. I never heard it before."

"Well, then?"

"But as soon as General Bnindagun started speaking it,
I immediately perceived what it had to be."

"And you taught it to yourself on the spot?"

"Sure, it's pretty easy once you realize all modern lan-
guages descended from that. Just like the proto-linguist
Morris Swadesh explained in the middle of last century.
You know, using lexicostatistics and glottochronology."

"Never heard any of those terms before."

"All you have to do is take all the common roots in all
current languages, then extrapolate back to their precursors and then the precursors to those precursors, all the
way back to where there are no more precursors. Then you
realize you've gone back to the original, the one with no
more precursors. Clear?"

"Clear as... clear as... as... clear."

"My dear Jacks, sometimes your linguistic prowess truly astounds me."

*Gotta hand it to Brexxie. He knows how to insult better
than anyone.* "Moving right along. What on earth was that
shiny mirage thing which suddenly appeared in the middle
of a blue sky?"

"Oh, that. That was a Schimmerplotz."

"Come again?"

"Let's go for a coffee and some Peanut M&Ms. I'm still
feeling weak. Stress releases the hormone cortisol and that
rapidly depletes serum glucose levels, leading to hypogly-
cemia. You know, what some people call the shakes. Coffee
will help my liver release glycogen and restore serum
euglycemia. And that's what I need right now before I try
and explain advanced concepts like this."

"Coffee it is, Brex. And hot chocolate for Sara. But if
you don't explain to me pretty quick what that
Shimmerdoofus thing is, I'm going to be really giving you
some shakes. The kind coffee won't help."

"Relax, Jacks! Don't hyper your hypertension any more
than you already have. I don't want my bodyguard to suffer

a coronary occlusion or myocardial infarction or some other vasovagal syncope and keel over on me. Besides, I need the time to think of how to simplify this enough for someone of your background to comprehend it. Maybe Sara here can help me."

"I'll try, Uncle Brexxie!" she said brightly as the three of us stood up. As we walked towards the Miramar Restaurant just to the northwest of Battery Park, she took the middle position between us, holding one of my hands and one of his. With my free hand I wiped away her final tear.

She smiled at me. "I love you, Daddy!"

"And I love you, sweetheart. More than you can ever know!"

2

The Schimmerplotz

At the Miramar Café on the western side of Manhattan island, facing the Hudson River, Brexxie ordered a triple foam maple syrup latte and a family-size pack of Peanut M&Ms. Sara requested a hot chocolate and a blueberry muffin.

I had plain black coffee and a scowl. My muscles ached from lack of exercise, as I had skipped my usual 90-minute gym workout and five-mile run in the morning to have this outing with two of my favorite people. There was only one other favorite person of mine, Momma Sara, my beloved wife, who stayed behind for a much-needed rest break with the family dog while we buddies took Little Sara out.

I knew Momma Sara badly needed a rest. She had been working night and day for weeks on her latest project, writing a book on physical therapy with her identical twin sister, an expert in the field. Tara knew PT but not much about writing. Sara knew everything about writing, but next to nothing about PT except for the key notions of stretching and strengthening muscles to keep all the body parts flexible and in balance.

It was a match made in heaven... or so it would seem. The writing of the book had gone well, and the publishing team was thrilled with it, but at times the Sara-Tara match seemed more as if it had been hatched in the other place

instead of heaven. In the final weeks of their editing process, Tara had stayed in the house with us nonstop to avoid
wasting time on daily commutes across the city and, after
working ten to twelve hours a day, loved nothing more than
playing pranks on us. She would dress up like Sara, put on
the little flourishes of her pose, facial expression, and accent, and then try to fool the rest of us.

Brex saw through it instantly. When Tara would prance
into a room pretending to be her twin, he would grimace
and look away in disgust. He refused to even comment out
loud.

Our dog BigBear would see a familiar person but quickly smell another and growl softly, the hairs on the back of
his neck bristling in confusion.

Little Sara would pretend to go along with the gag, call
Tara mommy, jump in her lap, and start to tell about her
day. Then in mid-sentence, she would lightly pinch the
woman's chin with her right thumb and forefinger—a distinctive Tara habit—and proclaim smartly, "I know it's you,
Auntie Tara."

I hated that game, for Tara played it to a whole different
level with me, sometimes by pretending to be my wife. She
would slip into the bathroom and come up behind me while
I was brushing my teeth, speak in that low, sultry voice,
and whisper something provocative in my ear such as,
"Ready for me, big boy?"

She never fooled me for an instant. When a man knows
his wife, I mean really knows her in the fullest sense, there
is a certain warmth in the touch, a particular mystical
quality of union into one new being, a unique responsive-
ness to each other's feelings and needs, which no one else
could possibly re-enact fully, but could at best only counterfeit. My Sara was a genuine hundred dollar bill; Tara was
Monopoly money, and I was the bank teller being asked to
accept both as equal.

Yet I couldn't just be rude. I wouldn't call her out or tell
her off. Instead I would pretend to accept the gag but then
brush her off with some jokey comment such as, "Not tonight, dear, I have a headache."

That usually did the trick. Tara would then laugh and
jump back and proclaim, "I got you, you big goof. It's me,
Tara!"

I couldn't wait for them to finish the project and for Tara to get the heck out and go home.

Sara almost kicked her in the rear on the way out. Well, 'almost' isn't quite the right word. She did kick at her backside and made gentle contact, but she put no force into it. "That's for trying to trick my husband! And I'd better not catch you trying to do it again!"

Tara just laughed. None of it had meant anything to her. Just clowning around; just tension relief.

But it meant something to Sara and the rest of us. It left a hot layer of tension floating in the atmosphere, like a warm weather front moving into a cool region, setting up the conditions for a possible thunderstorm to break out at any moment.

So Momma Sara had worked and slaved and put up with sibling rivalry for three weeks, two days, and 1.5 hours. This morning, when that door had shut behind Tara for the last time as she walked towards her taxi and a ride back to Manhattan, Sara gave me the exhausted look of a boxer who had just gone ten rounds, had avoided being knocked out, but now could barely stand.

I'd poured her a glass of wine, grabbed Little Sara and Brexxie, and headed for the door.

Now at the Miramar, resting a bit after our surreal adventure in Battery Park, the stress and lack of my usual exercise and tension relief was catching up with me as well. Right at the table as my best friend and little daughter munched on their treats, I stretched with a groan and almost bumped into an older woman seated behind me. "Excuse me," I said.

"No worries, mate," she said.

Australian. I loved Australia. Several times in the past few years they had paid for me to fly over there business class on Qantas Air and give their government security folks in the ASIO—the Australian Security Intelligence Organisation—a couple of days' instruction on how to improve security and prepare to protect their citizens from "The Big One."

Oh, my gosh, but they treated me like royalty, and I loved all of them, each and every one I had met, and would do anything to help protect that Land Down Under.

But still I sat in the Manhattan restaurant, and turning to my partner I muttered, "So give, Brexxie."

Instead of trying to explain the incident in the park, Brexxie silently mouthed to me, "She's Australian. I'm a sucker for that accent. I think I'm in love."

I had known Brex all my life, had grown up with him, had so often protected him from bullies even when we were kids, and we had developed our own ways of conversing surreptitiously. I mouthed back, "She's a bit old for you, isn't she? Probably old enough to be your mother."

He grinned, but it was a fake smile tinged with sadness. "When you look like I do, you can't be too picky."

Love. I knew Brex had always lacked the kind of female interaction he craved. I tried to change the subject. Out loud I said, "Quit stalling, Brexxie. Tell me what is going on."

"Okay, my dear Jacks. I've considered this and I think I can explain it if I start from a tangent and work my around to it indirectly, gradually homing in on the central point."

"Just so long as you get there, and before I finish my coffee," I mumbled. "Or I might directly work you around my big hairy fist."

Sara looked at me disapprovingly.

Brex noticed. "Don't worry, sweet girl. That's just your daddy doing his alpha male schtick again. He doesn't really mean it."

She looked relieved.

"Spill it, B."

"Okay. You know how over the centuries people have claimed to have had visions or visitations from the Great Beyond or space aliens or whatnot?"

"Of course."

"Well, that's what we had today."

"Maybe."

"No, indubitably, dear Jacks." He snickered before adding, "That means 'without doubt'."

I gave him a cross look that I hoped Sara wouldn't see. "More. Tighten the circle." Waiters were milling about, taking orders and delivering same. My Aussie friends behind me were rising and leaving and going to pay their checks on their way out.

"Of course, not everyone who has claimed visions has had this kind of experience for real. Some people have simply been ignorant or misinformed or misinterpreted a quite ordinary experience."

"You mean like folks claiming to see a UFO but it was really just an advanced and secret USAF experimental plane of some kind?"

"Okay. Then you are catching on. Maybe we can go deeper."

"Deepest deeper. My coffee is half gone."

I felt the sudden warmth of someone opening a pizza oven to bring out some customer's special request. The noise and hubbub around me died down as the delightful, delectable smells of something from the kitchen filled the air and probably made nearly everyone wish they had ordered something different.

"So some people misperceive a quite normal event and think it is supernatural when it isn't. There are also people who are just plain... how do I put this politely... mentally 'coocoo for Cocoa Puffs' and need to see a good psychiatrist."

"So they think they are seeing something that really isn't there at all."

"Indu—"

I scowled.

"Yep."

"But what we saw today was real. We all saw it. At least I saw part of what you two saw."

"Real as real can be."

"So what was it?"

"I can't quite get you to the center of the circle just yet. But that window into another dimension that suddenly appeared is called a Schimmerplotz."

"A Schimmerplutz?"

"No, plotz. Schimmerplotz."

"Which is?"

"A momentary collision of two dimensions within the space-time continuum."

I stared blankly, trying to grasp the significance of all this. Hardly ever could I understand what my best buddy Breslin Herndon was going on about. Imagine me being at the base of a pyramid, and the rest of the pyramid going up scores—no, hundreds of levels up towards some shining pinnacle. Breslin—AKA Brex or Brexxie—would be up there, studying the clouds, but I would still be waiting around impatiently at the bottom, chewing on my wet, unlit cigar, still trying to understand why the cab wasn't there...

Brex sighed. "Think of it as alternative highways criss-crossing all over the place, with overpasses and exits and service lanes all bearing heavy traffic. Sometimes there is a collision among all those vehicles. Often, like today, it is just a relatively harmless fender bender. But sometimes it can be quite serious. You know, like a multi-vehicle collision."

"Relatively harmless? It looked pretty serious to me when that weird character tried to kill you."

"Oh, that? That was nothing. When I say serious, I mean something like the vanishing of an entire civilization. Something like the loss of Atlantis or the Mayans or the ancient Sumerians and Akkadians."

"So who was that guy? You had a name for him. General something or other. Who is he and how do you know him?"

"General Bnindagun? I never saw him before today, but as I was forcing the Schimmerplotz to close on him, I glimpsed him in the past and present and future, all in different facets of the kaleidoscope, all at the same time... as a primitive warrior, as a modern man like us, and as a future ruler."

"That sounds downright eerie, like some kind of eternal man. What on earth is he up to, zooming through the space-time continuum?"

"You're better off not knowing about him or what he wanted. With any luck you'll never see him again. I mean, what is the likelihood of lightning striking the same place twice?"

"That happens all the time, Brex."

"Not really *all* the time. But I do see your point. The odds are approximately one out of 176,599 of that happening within an average human lifespan of 70.32 years."

"Approximately."

"Well, it is impossible to be more precise than that, for there are so many variables."

"Like what?"

"How one defines lightning, for example. Is it by size of the visible arc or the energy emitted or the absolute atmospheric temperature reached? And the precise area one is concerned with. Do we calculate the area under the curve by including a roundoff of the square miles of ocean along

the coasts? And the possibility of some lightning strikes going undetected. And, naturally, average lifespan is largely
an artificial statistical construct which changes all the time
and can never be calculated by mere humans to the exact
millisecond."

"So...?"

"So the most precise I can say at this moment in time is
probably 176,599, give or take an error margin of about a
hundred."

"But it happens is my point. So it could happen again."

"Indubi—"

I raised my right hand from my coffee mug. "So what
did General Bring-A-Gun say?"

"Bnindagun? You're really better off not knowing."

I clenched my fists, and Brexxie probably could see the
veins in my forearms starting to bulge.

Nervously he twittered, "Jacks, my dear boy, I really
can't say in front of Sara, you know."

I turned to her. "Sara, please go to the ladies room for a
couple of minutes."

She looked at me with a curious expression. "I don't
need to go, Dad."

"Just go powder your nose then."

Her look turned to puzzlement. "I don't have any powder, Dad."

"Sweetie, please go to the counter over there for a couple of minutes and pick out a treat to take home for Mom."

"I don't have enough money, Dad."

"Just tell them to add the cost to my bill, sweetie."

"Okay, Dad." She got up and wandered over to the
checkout counter, where there were all kinds of packaged
treats ready to go.

"Brex?"

"The general seemed quite angry about us observing his
secret plot being implemented. He swore he would kill me
and Sara both. And when I say swear, I never realized before how many curse words there were in Origanis. Those
primitive folks had quite the spicy vocabulary!"

My heart sank. "That's about what I figured."

He tossed his right hand into the air. "But the odds are
you won't ever see him again."

"I never play the odds, Brexxie. I like to be prepared for all contingencies. So I want you to tell me everything you know about this General Big-Gun."

"Okay."

Sara returned to the table with a small package. I took my last swig of coffee, left a twenty on the table, and went to the counter to pay the bill.

"Are you ready to go home yet, Sara?" I asked.

"Not yet, Daddy. I want to ride the SeaGlass Carousel again and maybe look out over the water and see the Statue of Liberty across the harbor."

We headed south on the Battery Park Esplanade again towards the bottom of Manhattan.

Five minutes later, after we had crossed three intersecting streets and reached a good lookout position beside the Hudson River, Sara piped up. "Dad?"

"What, darling?"

"I have to go to the bathroom."

I sighed.

3

General Bnindagun

At the SeaGlass Carousel, I bought three tickets for Sara and made sure she got on the fish-seat of her choice. I gave the operator a twenty to let Sara stay on three times in a row, and he seemed happy to take the money and do so. Once the music and the ride started, I grasped Brex firmly by the shoulder and drew him off to the side of the crowd waiting in line.

He seemed so tiny, frail, and light. Not much more than a scarecrow filled with straw. At least by weight. But I knew within that chest beat the heart of an Oz lion. The real deal. He had risked his life to save Sara and would do so again if need be.

He twisted loose from my grip, whimpering. "Ow."

"The general... now."

"Okay, Jacks, but you're not going to like this."

"How do you know him anyway?"

"Never saw him before today. But he had a name tag on his uniform in the future which was clear as day. Didn't you see it?"

"I stood at a bad angle... and it had to be in Origanis, not English... never mind... just proceed."

"He's a really bad pile of crap, Jacks. You don't want to mess with him."

"You're not usually so scatological, Brex."

"Well, this guy unnerves even me. And that takes a lot. I don't spook easily."

"So where's he from?"

"From here."

"You mean from an alternative dimension?"

"Bingo! Jacks, you may be starting to comprehend what we are up against. Just starting, mind you."

I noticed a couple of preteen punks in line eyeing us strangely, so I motioned for Brex to follow me further toward some nearby trees, but still within sight of the ride. "Given that his dimension is bumping into ours and might do so again, no matter what you say about lightning rarely striking the same spot twice, where does he think he is in his dimension?"

"My dear Jacks, it doesn't matter where he is now. It's a question of where he plans to go next. Remember his secret tunnel project that Sara spoke of?"

"One level of complexity at a time, Brexxie. Remember, I'm just a slugger. Get me to first base before you start talking about a home run."

"At this point, I'd be happy just to get you off the plate and moving in the right direction at all."

I growled again.

"I mean, at least lift your bat and try to hit something so you can take that first step. At least try to bunt."

"Scrap the baseball allusions. Season's over, and I don't even like baseball that much."

"That's only because you fail to appreciate the mathematical precision and theoretical purity of the game. It's a physicist's delight!"

I pursed my lips in silence and looked up to see Sara's second ride starting. That was pretty cool music, sort of a mix of relaxing new age and bouncy childhood fun. And the individual fish-shaped seats, made mostly of see-through but colored fiberglass, were enchanting.

Brex looked up at me as he might peer up at a looming statue in a museum. "See, you like football, where brawn counts more than brain. In football you don't really have to understand but one thing—how to bash and ram through your opponent, simply force on force, and may the strongest force win."

"Yeah, I like football. So what? You know I played fullback in high school and college."

"And you look even now as if you could play pro, but that's not my point. Do you even know the physics formula for force?"

"Nope, and I don't care to."

"It's actually one of the most elementary formulas in all the field of physics. It's force equals mass times acceleration."

"Mass. That's how big I am, right?"

"Not precisely, but that will do for now."

"And acceleration. That's how fast I am moving, right?"

"Sort of, as long as you express that in standard mathematical units. It's not simply velocity or speed, which is meters per second. It's the change in speed, meters per second per second."

Those punks I had noted earlier were still eyeballing us. One pointed at us and said something while the others laughed.

I grinned. "So if the mass of my tightly balled fist accelerates in a vector towards your head, a mighty force will be applied to said cranium, right?"

Brex gasped and took a step back. "Easy, big fellow. I'm not just teasing you. I'm trying to make a point."

"Yeah, I got it. The bigger I am and the faster I accelerate, the more force I have to smack down an opponent."

"My dear Jacks, don't take this so to heart. I actually have an important point. When the time comes, if it comes, force is the only way to deal with this general."

"And force equals mass times acceleration. I got it, Brexxie."

"Whew!" muttered Brex.

Sara's second ride was slowing down to its end. "So back to this General Big-Gun. Where does he think he is now?"

"General Bnindagun. Have you heard of Sumeria?"

"Of course. Most consider it the first genuine human civilization, after the prehistoric days of cavemen and wandering nomadic tribes and hunter-gatherers."

"Correct so far."

I smiled. As Sara's final ride started, she looked over and waved at us. I waved back.

"But civilization, with its creation of organized society, centralized cities, math and science and metallurgy, didn't just suddenly appear overnight after the prehistoric era."

"Obviously. There must have been centuries of transition."

"Yes. Thousands of years, actually."

I shrugged.

"Our current nemesis is from that early transition phase. That's where Sara and I encountered him. In Mesopotamia, the land in the Middle East around the Tigris and Euphrates rivers where Sumeria gradually built a true civilization with walled cities, a military with the most advanced weapons of that day, recordkeeping, royal libraries, and even mail delivery. But there were two major transitional periods before that."

I noted Sara's third ride would end soon and steered Brexxie back in that direction. "Which were?"

"First the Ubaid period, about eight thousand years ago."

"And then?"

"The Uruk period next, starting about six thousand years ago."

"And our guy Bag-A-Gun, who wants to kill you and Sara before you can divulge his secret, comes from the Ubaid period?"

"Bnindagun. Yes."

"And his secret tunnel is meant to transport him and his army to—?"

Brex looked worried. "I don't think he knows where he is headed. From what little I could observe, when I wasn't running all around his primitive ziggurat trying to help Sara escape, he does seem to be aware of Schimmerplotzes and how to access them."

"Do even you know that?"

We were back beside the exit from the ride now, and the music was winding down. Sara looked content and eager to come tell us about her multiple rides.

"Not yet. All my studies so far have indicated they are random, short-lived, and just happen on their own... sort of like lightning in that sense. They won't even be noticed unless people by chance just happen to be in the region at that moment."

"So the general doesn't know where he is going but is willing to explore and find out?"

"Yes."

"And the tunnel he is creating will give him some control over the duration of the Schimmerplotz so that he can feed his whole army through into the adjacent dimension?"

"Good, Jacks. You are finally catching up with me!"

Sara's third ride ended, and I knelt to receive her as she dismounted and ran towards the exit. "And you think he knows how to control the Schimmerplotz, but you don't?"

"Not yet. But this is going to be our next mission. Obviously."

"Obviously. And you think he might end up here, in our time and place?"

"As near as I could tell from overhearing things when I was in his world, he actually wanted to reach Sargon, King of the Akkadian Empire, who conquered much of Sumeria. Apparently Bnindagun and Sargon had a prior interdimensional conflict of some kind. But if he miscalculates, he could end up here."

Sara galloped past the gate. "Daddy, thanks so much!"

I hugged her as she ran into my arms. "Did you enjoy that, sweetie?"

"I did! It was the funnest of fun things all day." Turning to Brex, she said, "Uncle Brexxie, you should try it, too! I don't think Daddy could fit into one of those seats, but you could!"

He smiled and patted her on the head.

Just then the 'tween punks who had eyed us at least twice before were walking towards their seats for their turn. They were on the inside of the railing, quite near where we stood on the outside. One yelled out, "Hey, little girl! Which is your father—the egghead or the muscle man?"

Crossly, she looked at him and exclaimed, "Shut your mouth! They're both family."

A feeling of pride twirled through me.

Brexxie beamed at Sara.

4

The Bewildering

When we got home to our place on Long Island, it was clear Momma Sara had gotten the rest she needed. She said she had had a nap and a long soak in the tub with a glass or two of Château Roumieu 1996 Sauterne, with Alexa playing Bach. Then just prior to our return, she'd ordered delivery chicken fingers, French fries, and onion rings, and curled up on the couch sharing them with BigBear, our black Labrador retriever.

Little Sara ran to the couch and sprang up on it, hugging both mother and dog at once. BigBear licked both prodigiously.

Mom smiled and stretched. "Did you have fun, precious?"

"It was the bestest day ever, Mommy! Daddy let me ride the carousel four times and bought me hot chocolate and we saw the Statue of Liberty and Uncle Brexxie saved my life!"

Sara looked at me in alarm. "What?"

I moved quickly to join them all on the couch. "We had a little incident in Battery Park, but she's fine. Not a scratch." I pulled the small bag out of my jacket pocket. "Look, Sara wanted a blueberry muffin at the Miramar, and we got you one, too."

"Muffin? No, thanks. I want to hear about this so-called incident."

"It was scary, Mommy."

"What happened?"

I hedged. "It's nothing, Sara. She's fine."

She looked cross. "I'm not talking to you yet. I want Sara's side of this story first."

"Uncle Brexxie was teaching me all about the flowers in the Battery Gardens. You know, like foxglove, which produces digitalis."

Geez... is Brexxie her real father or what?

"Mommy, what's digitalis?"

"Never mind, dear. Then what happened?"

"This window thing just suddenly opened up in the blue sky, and somehow Uncle Brexxie and I fell through. There was some kind of army down there building a huge tunnel with some kind of train about to burst through a wall."

"What?"

"Then the bad leader saw us watching and sent everyone to chase us. We ran through this weird city made out of clay, and Uncle Brexxie led me up to the top of this high tower, a ziggabutt or something, and we jumped off it back into New York."

"A ziggurat," I said.

"What?"

"Then I ran to Daddy while the bad man tried to kill Uncle Brexxie. But he slammed the window shut on the bad man's arms and we all escaped."

"*What?*"

"It was super scary, Mom, but I'm okay now."

Momma Sara turned to me. "Did someone drop a tab of acid into her hot chocolate?"

"Negative on that, honey bunch."

"Did someone spike my Sauterne?"

"Certainly not, dear one, love of my life."

"Then I want an explanation. Brexxie, get over here!"

His eyes darted nervously back and forth. "Not now, Sara. I've got to go to my room and file a report with HQ."

His room. The safe room built by the Space Agency Cosmic Intelligence Group at a cost of one point three seven billion dollars beneath our house, to protect Breslin Herndon and his secret lab from fire; earthquake; flood; bullets, explosives and other conventional weapons; radiological, biological, and chemical weapons of mass destruction; nu-

clear weapons up to one megaton in strength; sonic, microwave, electromagnetic pulse, and other experimental weapons; wild animals, criminals, terrorists, foreign agents, and
other unsavory characters prone to violence; and now, it
seemed, from Sara's growing wrath.

As he departed our living room in haste, I yelled after
him, "I'm going to grab a can of Bud. Do you want one,
Brex?"

"Negatory, my dear Jacks. Catch you on the flip side."

I turned nervously towards Momma Sara. "My precious,
my sweet, you want another glass of Sauterne while I'm at
the fridge?"

"Better bring the whole bottle," she hissed. "And this is
the last time I stay home to rest while you two take Sara
anywhere."

5
HQ

After all the quizzing and griping stopped, Momma Sara eventually saw that our daughter was perfectly fine. It's not as if that were the first time she saw something strange while living around Brex, and it certainly wouldn't be the last. Little Sara was yawning but still quite chipper when we put her down for her afternoon nap.

Brexxie cautiously crept back up the stairs. "Is it safe now?" he whispered.

"No, let's go to your room."

We passed through the corridor, with its walls of eight-inch-thick steel, down 72 stairs in six flights of twelve each, around the body detectors, barriers, baffles, and booby traps which remained unarmed for the moment, and descended underground through the door which rivalled that of Fort Knox's gold repository for strength and security. I noted first the one part I really understood, the weapons room with its CQB rifles, 9mm Beretta pistols, RPGs, flamethrowers, and grenades—both fragmentation and flash-bang. Plus a few little gizmos Brexxie himself had invented for agents in the field who were outmanned and outgunned and running for their lives.

We had used some of those before on our special ops together, and they had saved our lives many times in the past. No matter what the situation, Brex usually could come up with something.

The rest of the rooms in his lab were filled with items I couldn't possibly understand, though I knew some of their names. He had a linear particle accelerator, a small 1.1-megawatt TRIGA (Training, Research, Isotope, General Atomics) nuclear reactor, a magna-powered laser generator, and electronic devices of all shapes, sizes, and descriptions. And commo gear of every possible kind to keep him in touch with HQ no matter what, or to track satellites and friendly agents in the field. Most of these items I knew nothing about and had never even seen him use.

My job had always been to protect him from enemies, not to share in his intellectual enterprises. I only came down here when we needed to talk privately or he wanted to show me something he was working on. Once in a while he asked for my input on how a field agent could use one of his creations for maximum impact. I certainly had the experience for that.

Breslin Herndon was the smartest scientist in the world and the powers that be in the government knew it. They would rather he worked within a top secret military base with layers upon layers of security.

Brexxie had done that in his early years, working at DARPA, but was fed up with government red tape and going through the bureaucratic hierarchy. One day he issued an ultimatum—give him what he wanted so he could do things for Uncle Sam his way, or no deal. He would enter the private sector, move to Silicon Valley, and become the first American trillionaire.

Uncle Sam gave in.

Brex was just too valuable to lose.

He paused beside a food dispenser resembling a bubble gum machine. "Want some Peanut M&Ms?"

"No, thanks. But I could use another Bud. Got any down here?"

"Nope. But I do have some bottles left of that Sam Adams Utopia that the president sent to thank us after our last successful caper."

"The one that costs a hundred fifty dollars a bottle?"

"Yeah. They age it in sherry, cognac, bourbon, and Scotch casks for up to eighteen years first. Then they add a touch of maple syrup before bottling. Want one?"

"Naw. I already drank my share the first week we got them. These are yours. Save 'em for a special occasion."

"Suit yourself."

"So what did HQ say?"

"You'll find it hard to believe."

"Try me."

"They don't want us to pursue this one."

"Why not?"

"Because they don't think the threat is imminent. They take that 'lightning won't strike twice' view more seriously than we do."

"But we're still going to pursue it, right?" I asked.

"Indu—"

I laughed. "It's a real word, Brexxie, you can use it. We will indubitably pursue it despite the lack of interest of our superiors... because—?"

"Not despite their lack of interest."

"No?"

"Precisely *because* of their lack of interest."

"So your spidey sense is tingling and telling you something is amiss?"

"Not that spidey bullcrap. Not my instinct, but my intellect."

"Meaning?" I asked, genuinely puzzled.

"Logic tells me they want this kept under wraps because they are in on it."

"But they don't want us to find out, maybe stumble onto the truth and let the secret out?"

"Correct, Agent Jack Rigalto. Someone higher up did something which triggered this weird Schimmerplotz today, maybe by deploying one of the cosmic field teams we've tangled with before."

"Oh, you mean like the Gemini Group, Iceman's team, or the Triangulators?"

"Exactly. Or maybe a new team we so far know nothing about."

"Someone in our agency may be experimenting with the space-time continuum, in other words, and trying to keep it quiet?"

"Correct. Though you and I perceive the danger of that, someone 'up there' is willing to risk it in the pursuit of some other end."

"So we are going to find out who, and what, and why."

"Exactly. You see, my dear bodyguard, you are the only one, despite not having my intellectual acumen, who has the right background to have any chance of keeping up with my line of thought. That's exactly why, when I threatened to retire and they offered me this set-up, I insisted on them putting you in charge of all my security. You are the one friend I can always count on!"

I started to prickle again, but just then Brexxie's private alarm went off and all the electronic security measures automatically started to kick in.

6

The Iceman Cometh

A muffled grinding of gears sounded as the massive main door to Brexxie's complex began automatically closing.

"No!" I barked. "Sara and Sara and BigBear are still up there."

Brexxie dashed to a nearby panel and pushed an override button. The door stopped moving in a half-open position.

Both of us looked up at the security screen—an enormous eight-by-eight foot flat-panel display with 64 squares, each single square foot of which showed the input from a different camera. The 64 cameras were hidden in all sorts of spots and provided overlapping views of every cubic inch of the space surrounding our place. Each single inch had at least three different cameras covering it, so that if one or two failed for some reason, there would always be a view of any given spot from another camera.

Except this time, three squares out of the 64 were all showing nothing but blank static. All three of the cameras focused on the back door approach. Someone who knew exactly where the key cameras were had knocked out precisely the three needed.

I pulled my 1911 Colt .45 semi-auto from its holster and cocked back the slide, loading a 230-grain full metal jacket cartridge into the chamber, and darted towards the stairs. I yelled back at Brex, "Check out the vid playback and see who or what took out those cameras!"

"On it! Turn on your earpiece!"

I reached up and did so as I, nearly out of breath, reached the top of the 72 stairs and burst back into the hallway towards our living room. I held my breath for a second, so as not to make a sound, and cautiously checked all directions as I stepped softly through the hallway.

Breathing again, I crept towards the bedrooms. Before entering mine and Sara's, I leaned my back against the wall and raised the point of my pistol. "Sara, get Sara and come to me."

"Can't," she whimpered.

I could hear BigBear's muffled growls. Sounded as if someone had thrown a quilt over his head.

"Why not?" I blurted out, already knowing the answer.

"Because I have them," came a deep and robust—and also very familiar—male voice.

The Iceman!

Then Brexxie's voice softly came through my earpiece. "Got them. You're not going to like this. Three guys in black tactical garb with CQB rifles slung over their shoulders and holding paintball guns, each one taking out one of the cameras at the same time. No identifying marks on their garb, but gait pattern analysis reveals the leader is our old friend The Iceman."

"I know," I whispered. "They've got my—our—family."

"Agent Jack Rigalto, it is my sworn duty officially to inform you that my orders in such a case are to seal the great door so that enemies cannot penetrate this classified facility."

"Do it!" I hissed. "Do what has to be done." *Glad Brex is secure but now there's no one to watch my six as I face these goons.*

"Sorry, my dear friend. Out here."

"Out."

When preparing the Herndon secret lab and safe room below, the agency had also modified my house above to add security while making it appear as just another normal house in this exclusive neighborhood on Long Island. *Iceman knew where the cameras were, but does he know about the secret panels as well?*

I crept slowly backwards towards the fireplace, keeping my eyes and ears trained on the open bedroom door. When I reached the mantelpiece, I touched the top edge of the frame holding the president's official signed photo. It took me a second to feel for the special button and press it.

Without a sound, the cold fireplace rotated 180 degrees, and I stepped into the hidden crawlspace which connected with all the rooms in the main house, our family residence. Dark in here, but no cobwebs, as Momma Sara frequently cleaned the area and Little Sara loved to play hide 'n seek in there.

I reached the bedroom mirror, which was one way and allowed me to see in without being observed from the other side.

My two Saras sat on the bed while one goon aimed his rifle at them. Our enormous purple and gold quilt, hand-made by my late mother when I graduated from LSU, lay on the floor, suddenly coming to life with a large creature struggling to get out from under it. *BigBear is going to smother to death if I don't get him out of there fast.*

Iceman—I could tell by the broad shoulders and tree-trunk-like legs—had his rifle aimed at the entrance near where I had stood moments ago.

The third gunsel had his rifle aimed right into the mirror; right into my face.

I could feel goosebumps rising on my arms.

They know about the secret panels!

Clearly he was waiting for me to make some sound or give away my position by exposing a light, then he would send a volley of 5.56mm bullets through the mirror right into my head.

Very cautiously, I crept further away instead, into the bathroom where we had a huge round tub with whirlpool nozzles and a separate shower.

I pressed the button behind the shower, and its back wall, tiles and grout and all, rotated halfway, and I slipped in.

The man at the mirror shouted "I hear him, boss!" at the same time he released a volley which shattered the mirror into a thousand pieces.

Bad luck for you. Sure doom for you.

In the split second it took for me to reach the bathroom door into the bedroom, that goon had already leapt through the ruins of the mirror into the concealed crawlspace.

I fired my .45 three times into the area where I thought he was running, but I heard no grunts of pain. I had about a second and a half before he outflanked me and I would be surrounded by enemies. I leapt into the room and took out the man guarding my girls with a single shot to the head.

Iceman fired back at me, unaiming, as he retreated and burst through the open bedroom door out to the living room where I had been just moments ago.

Little Sara screamed and clapped her hands to her ears to muffle the intense gunfire booms. Momma Sara sprang from the bed and freed BigBear. That put him in more danger, because he would likely chase one of the felons and get shot to blazes.

"Heel!" I commanded BigBear, and he bounded to my side, panting heavily, as I stepped quickly into the room, hoping to keep from getting outflanked. I turned to my daughter. "Get under the bed! Now!"

She scurried there in a flash.

With my left hand, I retrieved my .380 backup semi-auto pistol from its ankle holster and tossed it to my wife, a trained marksman who often worked out at the range with me.

"Too weak," she muttered, dashing to her nightstand and retrieving her .357 Magnum revolver. With a look of resolve on her face, she now had one gun in each hand, looking up at me for guidance.

"Stay here and protect Sara. And keep a sharp eye out for that punk in the crawlspace. All the panels are open."

BigBear and I snuck towards the bedroom door and he growled in warning. Iceman had to have his rifle trained on that spot, just waiting for me to show myself.

Iceman yelled out, "Listen to me, Special Agent Jack Rigalto. I have a message for you, and things will turn out better for all of us if you pause to hear me out first."

What kind of idiot do you think I am? You hold my wife, daughter, and dog hostage, then try to shoot me down?

I grabbed a jacket from its coat-hanger on the back of the door and tossed it through the opening. A long burst of automatic fire left it tattered, with at least two dozen bullet holes before it touched the floor.

At the ear-shattering sound of Sara's .357 behind me, I whirled to see her shooting into the bathroom. No sign of a body. Assuming she'd heard or seen something before firing, that punk must have pulled back from the doorway and was well shielded somewhere in the bathroom.

We were getting flanked!

Before I could decide my next move, I felt the whole floor vibrate and shiver, like some pitiful creature underdressed in an arctic icestorm. A bright light filled the living room and grew more dazzling by the second, like a nuclear sun rising over Hiroshima. Finally a noise like crashing nearby thunder filled the room.

Then darkness. Silence. Just a tiny breath of rotting wind smelling as if it had passed over a septic tank before reaching my nostrils. The sharp ionization in the air still crackled to the point where my arm hairs stood on end.

I took a breath and leapt into the room, somersaulting halfway across the empty space and coming up to a crouch, with my .45 aimed at the wall where I thought Iceman had been hiding.

No Iceman.

Just a pillar of salt where I thought he must have been.

At least it looked like a pillar of salt. I couldn't help but think of Lot's wife when I saw it, the way she would have looked after turning back longingly to her home in Sodom and Gomorrah when God rained fire and brimstone on those wicked cities near the Dead Sea.

I looked in the other direction, towards the hall leading to Brexxie's lab entrance, and saw him standing there with a grim but satisfied look on his face. His hands held what looked like some kind of ray gun from a sci-fi movie, with flourishes and baffles angling up in all directions, and the tip of its flared barrel still glowed a curious blue-green.

That left only one attacker to worry about.

Suddenly the sounds of a major skirmish from the bedroom. I could hear at least three weapons roaring simultaneously. Automatic rifle fire. A high-powered pistol and a low-powered one, with fire alternating rhythmically.

I dashed to the door. Momma Sara knelt beside the bed, its sheets and padding throwing up a hail of ripped cloth and foam chunks, raining down on her like confetti at a downtown Fifth Avenue parade.

I still had a couple of rounds in my .45, but needed a full load for this final assault. I quickly exchanged the old mag for a fresh one and chambered a round, somersaulted back into the bedroom, and emptied all of it into the torso of the final punk as he charged from the bathroom.

Panting, I checked for pulses on the two corpses there. None. "BigBear, get little Sara!"

The huge dog yelped and shook his tail eagerly as he crept under the bed to join her.

I stepped back into the living room to check the pillar of salt. It was still smoking and too hot to check for a pulse, as if blocks of inert minerals were even capable of a pulse.

Brex still stood in the doorway as before, but the experimental rifle was now sagging in his grip. He looked weak, as if about to collapse.

"Brexxie!" I shouted in astonishment. "I thought you were hiding in your bunker!"

"And leave my best friend—and family—to their fate? I think not! I did my sworn duty by sealing the door to the secret chamber, but by golly, no orders said I had to be on the inside when I did it. I'm not abandoning my family for any orders by any power on this earth!"

"Hooray for Uncle Brexxie!" yelled little Sara, her hands locked around the big dog's neck as he practically dragged her into the room.

Brex sagged to the floor and I bounded to his side, taking the rifle lest he drop it and possibly set it off again.

His eyes half shut, he croaked, "Weak... about to pass out... Peanut M&Ms, quick!"

Momma Sara was standing among us now, both pistol barrels still emanating thin trails of gunsmoke. "I'll get 'em, Brexxie. Hold on!"

7

Dead Men Can Tell Tales

Momma Sara was in the other room, fuming about all the mess. "Who's going to clean up all this blood and gore and this horrid, weird statue thingy? Who's going to repair all the damage? And my best winter coat that my mom gave me with a million holes in it!"

Brex sat on the living room couch, wrapped from head to toe in a thick Taiwanese blanket colored with huge swirls of green and orange and pink. He was sipping hot cocoa from a steaming mug and munching on M&Ms. "Don't worry, Sara, I'll call The Cleaners!"

"The cleaners?" she shouted. "No cleaners on earth can fix all this mess."

"These ones can. They're from the agency. They'll spend a million dollars on it if I tell them to."

Alarmed, I held up a hand like a stop sign. "Whoa, Brexxie! Wait a minute. Weren't these thugs *from* the agency? Sent to nix us because you raised the alarm about the Schimmerplotz?"

"I don't think so, Jacks. I think these guys worked for someone else who intercepted my messages."

"Well, you may be right. The Iceman never worked with us, as far as I know."

Brex nodded. "There was always something odd about him and his team. They never seemed quite on our side or any enemy's side either. Not lions or gazelles; more like freelance hyenas, watching and laughing on the wayside until one side had won and they could creep in, laugh some more, and share in the spoils. I never knew exactly whom they worked for."

I shrugged, feeling a little foolish. "It's a shame all three are now ghost riders in the sky. We'll never get any information out of them now."

"Don't be so sure," Brex said. "Sometimes dead men *do* tell tales."

"You've got something in the lab which might help?"

"Maybe. I mean, I've got stuff in the lab. Whether it will yield useful information is another matter."

"You know what, Brexxie?"

"Yeah?"

"I think our joint survival today is a cause for celebration. Do you mind if we break open and share one of your final bottles of Sam Adams Utopia?"

"Go ahead, buddy. Be my guest."

I retrieved it and came back with one bottle, but three glasses. I offered one to him.

He shook his head. "Naw. With all this chocolate in my mouth, it will taste like crap."

I put his empty glass down on the coffee table and looked over at Momma Sara. "Come over here, sweetie. Let's have a toast."

She'd calmed down and now just seemed happy we were all still alive and unhurt, and she smiled at what I held in my hands. "Ooh, another one of those extraordinary beers from the president? You know, it's nice when a president appreciates people fighting to save America rather than those wishing to diminish it!"

I poured half the bottle into her glass and handed it to her, then emptied the rest into my glass and placed it on the table until I could return with a ginger ale for Little Sara.

"Can I smell yours first, Daddy?"

"Sure," I said, handing it to her. "This is the most expensive beer made in America. It's very special."

She accepted my glass but offered it first to BigBear. He sniffed cautiously at it but then turned his head away in disgust. "He doesn't like it, Daddy, so it must not be good."

"What do you think of it, Sara?"

She sniffed and her eyes flew open wide. "Maple syrup, Daddy! But the rest of it is so yuck!"

I laughed. "Now let's have a toast. To Brexxie, friend of all and man of the hour!"

Brexxie smiled and clicked his hot cocoa mug with my glass, then Momma Sara's, then Little Sara's.

Two hours later, while Sara and I were still directing The Cleaners, Brex re-emerged from his lab. "Big news, buddy!"

"What did you find?"

"Come down and see."

In the monitoring room, he paused beside the flat-panel display. All 64 cameras were working again, all showing various views of the house and grounds. He pushed a button and the entire screen instead lit up with a satellite view of the earth. "Remember those spy satellites I designed?"

I nodded. "Of course. But I thought once you turned over the plans, that was the end of your involvement."

"Not quite," and he smiled. "I kept a back door open in case I ever needed to use them myself." He fiddled with controls until the view zoomed in on our house as seen from above.

"Pretty cool, Brexxie."

He held a laser pointer and aimed at the screen. "See that van? That's how they got here." He pressed something, and the video showed three dark figures emerging from the van, one with a distinct muscular shape and gait. More like a football center stomping into the opposition than like the two slender and fast sprinters on either side of him. The three had CQB rifles slung over their backs and held only paintball guns. Within seconds they had separated, reached their positions at the back, and covered three camera lenses with dark goo.

"Where's that van now?"

"Back at Regional HQ in Manhattan. One of The Cleaners took it in for analysis."

"So it does seem more and more that you are correct, and that this recent assault wasn't ordered by our bosses."

"So it would appear. But I am suspecting there is at least one inside man at HQ who worked to tip off this hit team. They got here just minutes after my first contact and warnings."

"So where did these guys come from?"

"Just what I was wondering," said Brex, "so I followed the satellite feed in reverse and tracked the van back to where it started an hour before they got here."

He pushed a button and I could see the van and all its adjacent traffic moving in reverse. Brex highlighted the van and we watched it join then leave various threads of traffic, all in reverse.

"I don't need to watch the whole track. Just tell me where they started."

"You're not going to believe it."

"At this point I'll believe anything. Tell me."

"At the UN headquarters, between 42nd and 48th Streets, along the East River."

I mused, "That's not so surprising. Some foreign power or powers may be involved in something like this."

"True, that is not so surprising in and of itself. But guess which diplomat can be seen escorting these three to the van?"

"Russian or Chinese? Maybe Iranian? Possibly Cuban?"

"No, no, no, and no."

"Don't waste my time, Brex. Just tell me."

He smiled a sardonic grimace. "A guy named Jacques Bouchard from Quebec. Part of the Canadian delegation."

"So, what do we do next? Go to the UN and confront this guy?"

"No, we watch and wait. Patience, my dear friend, patience. Let him make the next move."

"That shouldn't take too long. He probably already knows his three goons didn't succeed."

"Oh, he does. Believe me, he does," said Brex. "I've been monitoring his communications, and he and his little cabal are starting to panic."

"Cabal? Who else is in on this?"

"An undersecretary from France and one from Germany."

"These are our allies, Brex! Not enemies!"

"Well," he said, "those governments certainly are allies, but that doesn't mean they can't possibly have rotten apples in otherwise good barrels, rogues secretly working for someone or something else other than their own governments."

"And who or what might that be?"

"Some globalist New World Order group or another."

"Yeah, that makes sense. But which one?"

"That's what we've got to find out."

"Count me in, Brex. Count me in."

"I always do, dear Jacks. I always do."

8

The East River

I wanted to get a closer look at the spot on the UN compound that Brexxie had spoken of. Technically, the compound was extraterritorial and under the governance of the United Nations itself, and not part of U.S. soil. We couldn't legally just go barging in there.

So we hired the owners of the *Manhattan II* cruise boat and chartered them for a run around the whole island of Manhattan, starting from the small port on the western edge of Manhattan on the Hudson, Pier 62 in the Chelsea district, proceeding north and then around to the East River, then south again, rounding the southern tip of Manhattan where we had first seen the Schimmerplotz in Battery Park. The boat normally took tour groups on that loop twice a day and shouldn't arouse suspicion by adding a third run just for us. In addition to brunch cruises and dinner cruises and sightseeing cruises, they often catered to special events such as corporate leadership award ceremonies and wedding parties.

The tour operators had no idea what we were up to, and doubtlessly assumed we were just two rich tourists who wanted to ride on a motor yacht patterned after the old millionaires' yachts of the Great Gatsby Roaring 20s era. It was 100 feet long and had glass paneling all around the main cabin to offer unobstructed views. It was an awfully big

space just for two weirdly matched partners, but none of
the staff seemed to mind having a greatly reduced number
of clientele to serve. In fact they all looked quite relieved at
the prospect of a light and easy work session.

As we pulled away from the pier and chugged up the
Hudson, that glorious Manhattan skyline came into view. I
could see the Empire State Building not more than a mile
away, then the tops of the ritzy buildings along Route 9A,
the skyscrapers west of Central Park, then the nearby Riverside Park along the western shore of Manhattan proper
and the General Grant National Memorial. As we rounded
the north end of the island, we shifted to the Harlem River
and kept curling around 'til we were on the east side of
Manhattan, descending until the East River merged and
made the whole channel that much wider.

Except for carrying our own oddly large and heavy
briefcases, both containing special items Brex had prepared
and packed just in case 'lightning' struck twice, we fully
played the part of rich guests, and let them wine and dine
us with rock crab dip made with Hollandaise sauce, filet
mignon steaks cooked to order, and a cheese plate including Pappilon Roquefort, Emmentaler Swiss, and Muranda
aged British cheddar, all washed down with French Veuve
Clicquot Champagne.

I enjoyed the fine dining as we waited for the UN complex to come into view, just south of the Ed Koch
Queensboro Bridge, but my partner wasn't that happy.

"I wish they served Peanut M&Ms, too," grumbled Brex.

"Shush, Brexxie. A little protein won't hurt you. You're
too thin and scrawny as it is."

"I don't want protein. I need glucose for my cerebral
neurons. You know, brain cells are the only cells in the
whole body which cannot store glucose and require a
steady influx from the bloodstream to function. And my su-
per-charged brain burns up glucose like a California forest
fire in the dry season."

"So, eat some more of those Bavarian rye crackers from
the cheese plate. Those will raise your blood sugar."

"I will," he said, grabbing a couple of crackers plain and
sipping his glass of ice water. "Now you, my big friend, you
need all the meat protein you can eat to maintain those
huge muscles. Rich thick, juicy steaks so raw the meat still

moos when you cut into it. Big bloody piles of red, red meat. Your system is based on meat and protein and muscle, mine on neurons and glucose."

I laughed at him. "It takes all kinds, doesn't it, buddy?"

"If you were really my buddy, you'd get me some Peanut M&Ms."

"Well, now that you ask, and asked so nicely, as a matter of fact I do have some on me."

His frown turned to consternation. "Don't tease me, Jacks, I'm not in the mood. My brain is seriously depleted of glucose."

"Well, after what happened on our last outing, I wanted to make sure we were prepared for any contingency. If you got stuck in Sumeria again during the sixth millennium B.C., I figured we couldn't find any Peanut M&Ms just when you might need them most." I reached into my pocket and pulled out a small yellow package.

His look of consternation turned to astonishment and then a big grin. He eagerly grabbed the pack from my hand, ripped it open, and started tossing the colorful nuggets back. "Thanks, my dear Jacks. You can have the rest of my steak." He pushed the plate towards me.

"Thanks, Brexxie, but no thanks. You ordered yours well done. That is a travesty for fine aged beef like this. I like mine rarer than rare."

"Just like the Neanderthal you are."

"Just like the caveman I am. I kill the woolly mammoth, cut off a chunk, throw it in the fire 'til it starts to smell good, poke my spear into it to retrieve it, and then start eating while the blood oozes down my cheeks."

Brex looked revolted. "You paint a very unpleasant picture of Neanderthal life, Jacks."

"Pleasant or unpleasant is up to interpretation. But truthful it is, whether you like it or not."

He ate another rye cracker and topped it with a yellow M&M while I finished my bloody steak.

We were passing Roosevelt Island on our left now and slipped under the Queensboro. Soon the Turtle Bay area came into view, and then the distinctive shape of the 39-story Secretariat Building of the UN complex.

I saw something and my heart sank. "See that?"

Brexxie burped up a strong odor of chocolate that could be smelled even across the table. "Excuse me."

I just grinned.

"I saw it minutes ago but hoped it would disappear before you saw it."

A glistening window in the blue sky, directly ahead of us, over the river, seemed to grow larger and more sparkling as our yacht approached.

When it lay only ten yards ahead of us, Brex flipped open his briefcase and whispered, "Hold your breath, Jacks, and put on those mitts I made especially for you."

I opened my briefcase, too, and got them out just in time, just as the entire boat shivered through the Schimmerplotz and left us falling a few feet with a plop into the Euphrates River of ancient Mesopotamia. Brex had shown me modern photos of the area which he and Little Sara had been shunted into, so I recognized the basic geography, but this was clearly more primitive than what was seen in the modern pics. I could see on the shore nearby some irrigated fields with rows of wheat being tended by peasants dressed in animal skins, a small clearing with a number of mud brick huts and a couple of open campfires, a huge area of clay being formed into sun-dried bricks, and a giant tower under construction just beyond that. The base of the tower was quite long and wide, massive and high. Atop that stood another, much smaller layer made with the same basic design. Yet a third sprouted on top of that, and a fourth atop that, from which sprung a half-finished temple with huge log and stone pillars.

What alarmed me most, however, were the small riverboats racing towards us as fast as sails and paddles would allow.

The tour operator looked confused and grabbed his microphone for the loudspeaker system, but was apparently so rattled he forgot to turn it on. "Don't be alarmed, folks," he yelled without amplification over a growing roar of war cries. "We have everything under control."

"No, he doesn't," I whispered.

"But I do," said Brex. "I figured as we got closer to the source of the problem, namely the UN, it might appear again, and this time I'm ready. Get out your time prod while you still can."

The water swirled and splashed near us, and I looked over the side. A large school of carp fled the churning paddles of the warcraft surging our way. I looked up towards the armada, now rapidly gaining on us, the ascending chorus of war cries filling the air, punctuated by barked orders.

I put on my electromagnetic mitts, feeling a bit like Michael Jackson getting ready for a concert. They were shiny and metallic, quite thick and heavy, but also very flexible. I pulled from my case something which resembled a collapsible nightstick, flicked my wrist, and it shot out to its full length of about three feet. At its tip was a pincer mouth rim resembling a stun gun. I hadn't seen it in action yet, but I knew after one glance that I didn't want to be on its receiving end.

At least two hundred warriors were now so close I could almost smell them. Some still paddled, but others stood at the prows, ready to board our craft.

Armed and ready, I turned back to Brex, now similarly attired. "When this is over, if these mitts work and we survive, you are going to have to explain to me how they work."

"It won't help if I do. You'll never understand it no matter what I say. There just aren't words simple enough for you to understand which can adequately explain it."

"Well, if you are as bright as you think you are, then you should be able to come up with some!"

"Blah, brugduh, blump!"

"What's that?"

"The words I just thought of that are elementary enough for you to understand."

"That's bullcrap! Those aren't real words!"

"It's the same level of communication as if you were explaining to BigBear how dog food is made at the factory. You could talk all day, but all he would hear would be 'blah, brugduh, blump.' Sometimes verbal communication across species simply doesn't work!"

"You and I are from the same species, Brex."

"Really? That's what you really think?" He paused and looked through the window. "He sees us. Here he comes. Get ready!"

The bow of our boat dipped as dozens of feet leapt aboard from the canoes.

"You mean General Bring-A-Gun?"

"See what I mean, Jacks? You don't understand Origanis at all. And neither can you understand my theories on celestial mechanics and interdimensional collision. But I can assure you of this—we will be in a giant pile of BigBear droppings if you don't do exactly as I say!"

I started to object, but just then the blade of a swinging battle-axe passed barely two inches over my head.

9

The Euphrates River

"I don't think your General Big-Gun likes us very much, Brex." I wielded my time prod like a sword and blocked the barbarian's next axe swing. His weapon had at least ten times the bulk and weight of mine, like a huge oak branch versus a thin reed, and I thought the force of his would shatter mine at once. Instead, mine seemed about one hundred times stronger, despite its slenderness, and readily held its own. In fact, his bounced right off mine, and he moaned with both pain and surprise.

"Bnindagun. His name is General Bnindagun. You're only going to make him madder if you keep making fun of his name."

"He's mad as a hornet as it is, Brex. How can I make him any madder?"

"Don't try and find out."

Spears of wood with sharpened bone blades flew towards us, and dozens more troops in full battle gear with Neolithic copper swords and flint knives clambered aboard, so many at once that the yacht started rocking.

The tour guide with the microphone threw it at the nearest attacker. "Abandon ship!" He leapt overboard and splashed into the murky water.

The waitress and bartender instead ducked behind the bar and started throwing liquor and champagne bottles at any barbarians who approached.

I used a chair in my left hand to trip two Ubaidians and whack a third one across the skull. Brex, fueled by the recent infusion of M&M energy, nimbly ducked and bobbed and made his way to a wall which would cover his back. But while dealing with the throng, we were pushed further and further apart.

"If we get separated, Jacks, make for the ziggurat and look for the interdimensional tunnel!"

"How?" I yelled, dodging a spear thrust, wrenching the spear out of my assailant's hands, knocking him out with the blunt end, and skewering a man behind me with the sharp end. "There's too many of them!"

"The mitts! Use your mitts! I've got to send these terrified Americans on board back to our century before they get killed in this one!" He headed for the bar to help the shrieking girls cowering there.

Spear points from all directions headed for my face. Instead of ducking, I swept my left mitt back and forth in front of me, and any spear I touched instantly vaporized. With my right hand, I used the time prod more aggressively, whipping at any native who drew near. As soon as my prod made contact with flesh, said flesh sparked like a death row murderer in the electric chair, quivered and shook, then fell lifeless to the deck.

"The girls are safe!" Brex cried. "And the captain and first mate. I'm going to get the tour guide who's in the water and head for shore. Join me!"

Kicking and thrashing with mitts and prod, I slowly worked through the crowd towards Brex. Both of us were bloody from nicks, cuts, and shallow stabs sustained from blades we hadn't vaporized in time. I hoped none were poisonous, but in this day and age, even just dirty ones could be dangerous by causing an infection, if we were stuck here without antibiotics. And everything smelled and looked dirty.

I grabbed Brex by the elbow and hustled him to the side of the yacht near a shallow draft sailboat being held in place by a lone Ubaidian. He took one look at my fierce face and jumped into the water, diving beneath and swimming for his life. I tossed Brex onto the boat, and he leaned over to assist the sputtering tour guide, who still splashed in the waves.

Several natives leapt at me simultaneously and I thrashed wildly back at them, spinning around and turning to inert matter any flesh I could touch. Then I jumped into the boat and used all the force in both my legs to push us away from the yacht, just as the tour guide pulled himself over the side of the sailboat with Brex's feeble assistance.

"It's not working any longer, Jacks! I can't send this dude back like the others."

"What's not working?"

"My time boomerang." He held up something resembling a three-dimensional Moebius strip. "It worked fine on the other four, but it must have run out of power."

"Out of power? *Out of power*? You're the smartest man in the world, and you forgot to bring batteries to recharge it?" I could feel my face flushing.

"I did bring batteries."

"Then where are they?"

"In my briefcase."

"And where's that?"

"Still on the yacht."

I looked back at it, some hundred or so feet behind us now. Dozens of Ubaidians still milled about, whooping war cries and victory shouts, and shaking spears at us as the little sailboat slipped further away. Several natives lit fires all along the boat, the flames of which soon grew and merged together. As the yacht receded further and further into the distance, flames leapt all about it and natives began to plop into the water to get away.

I felt a low, lingering dread as the yacht began to sink, our two briefcases along with it.

With dismay written all over his face, the tour operator stared at us both. "Is this a nightmare?"

"No," said Brex. "It's all very real."

"Am I on drugs?"

"Not so far as I know."

"Is it a terrorist attack?"

"Not yet, but it may be one in the making."

The poor man started retching and then leaned over the side to throw up this morning's food. Seems he had stone crab, steak, and the cheese plate, too. I turned away and tried to suppress my own nausea.

A mosquito buzzed in my ear and I swatted it away. We were getting near the shore.

"Where are my friends?" the poor man gasped between heaving glubs.

"They're back home, safe and sound," reassured Brex. "Try not to worry. We're going to get you home, too, just as soon as we can."

"If I'm not home, then where am I?"

"You don't want to know."

I managed a croaking sort of laugh. "Believe him, friend. You really don't want to know."

"Who are you guys, anyway?"

"Relax, pal," said Brex. "We're from the U.S. government. We're here to help."

"Oh, my gosh!" exclaimed the man. "I'm a goner now for sure!"

I guffawed at that. "Go on, Brexxie boy, give him something a little more optimistic. Who are we really, bro? I mean, who are we *really*?"

Brex sighed. "The simple and plain truth is that I'm Dr. Brains and he's Mr. Brawn."

At that the poor man almost chuckled. He eyed each of us up and down, and his face seemed to relax a bit. "That fits! That's what you two are—Brainiac and Hercules. I can see it. And I'm glad you two are on our side. That is, compared to whatever that other side even is. I feel like I'm in a Tarzan movie or something, but this doesn't look like Africa."

More mosquitoes, and the water was so shallow I could see minnows flitting about just below us and almost make out the river bottom. "It's not," I said. "It's Asia. Mesopotamia, to be exact."

"You mean those guys are Iraqis? They don't look like it."

"Like I said, you don't want to know."

I heard war cries rising in the distance again, growing louder, and looked back at the final flickers of flame on the sinking yacht. Still near there, but rapidly heading our way, were a dozen small riverboats, each filled with more angry warriors yelling their lungs out.

I looked in the other direction. The nearest point of the shore lay not more than fifty yards away, but the village was still about a quarter mile away, with the ziggurat not far behind that. Could we reach that before the general's crowd caught up with us?

I glanced at the deck of the little sailboat, hoping for useful gear. Bingo! I handed a wet paddle to the tour guide. "What's your name, anyway, friend?"

"Bill Higgins."

"Besides being a tour operator, what's your story?" I asked.

"I used to be a professional athlete. Until I got injured."

I cocked my head. "What sport?"

"Lacrosse."

Brex grimaced. "Well, there's not a lot of that here. Not in this time and place."

I tried to reassure the poor man with a wink. "Here, Bill, paddle for your life. We're headed for that tower over there." Next I handed one to Brex and grabbed one for myself as well.

Brex looked exhausted. "I'm getting weak again, buddy. I hope you brought some more of those M&Ms!"

"Later. Paddle now. You've got to have a functioning liver in there somewhere to get you through a momentary lack of glucose consumption."

He grunted. "Of course I do. Mine produces and stores what would be a normal amount of glycogen if I was home lounging around the pool sipping mai tais and watching you mope about like a lazy silverback gorilla, and glycogen releases glucose. But when my brain is running on all one hundred twenty-eight cylinders trying to process everything like a Cray supercomputer so that we can get out of this alive, I usually run out of liver glycogen in about thirty minutes and then hit the wall. Remember—"

"I know, your mighty brain burns glucose like a blast furnace." My paddle, at least, continued to splash, and we were close enough to shore to smell it, the gritty smell of dust and clay, and a fainter smell of the fertilized fields beyond.

Bill looked him over between strokes. "I can see that..."

The two of them paddled feebly, but once I kicked mine into gear, the little boat surged forward, parallel to shore, like a filly at the Kentucky Derby straining for first place. Beads of sweat formed on my forehead, as I hadn't paddled this hard since unsuccessfully trying out for the Olympic rowing team a few years ago.

I wasn't even sure which would be the best way for us to die. Caught by the savages behind us and quickly cut to pieces? Or perhaps captured and hauled for human sacrifice to the temple that was as yet incomplete, atop the ziggurat looming larger and larger as I paddled fiercely towards it?

In the end, it wasn't my decision to make.

We reached the shore only two hundred feet ahead of the general's warriors pursuing us down the Euphrates River, the one which, with the Tigris River to the east, defined the boundaries to ancient Mesopotamia. Well, ancient as defined by me when I grew up in modern America. But to these dudes living right now, back about eight thousand years ago from my perspective, these *were* modern times.

These dudes now, when not chasing and trying to kill us, thought of this very time as the modern time. For them, that is. They loved their king and their improved lifestyle, living in man-made villages now instead of natural caves or thatched lean-tos, enjoying their marital rites and rights, watching their children grow and wondering why the new generation didn't properly respect what had come before, marveling over how the young'uns traipsed around among themselves and dissed everything which had happened before their births, each one looking for new grunts and pals and thrills... and the occasional drumbeat and war dance echoing down from the distant hills.

All very amusing to contemplate until we reached the muddy shore, our consciousness informed by another eight thousand years of civilizational advance, only to face what we considered primitive savages, only to find them seeing us as weird alien invaders, perhaps from a distant planet, perhaps sent from the various gods they worshipped or despised, perhaps figments of their own fevered imaginations as they sat in sweat lodges and munched on hallucinogenic plants.

Whichever.

As we approached the reed-lined riverbank, I could see the farmers still bent over and laboring in the fields, weeding the rows of wheat, cleaning out the irrigation channels, raising and then lowering the thick wooden barriers that controlled the flow of water. These laboring folks in loin-cloths and with dirty bare feet paid no attention to us.

But their overseers and guards, wearing helmets and their feet shod with leather boots, folks wielding authority and weapons, heard the cries of their fellow citizens in the boats behind us and paid quite a bit of attention.

Someone high up in the chain of command on shore barked out an order, and a bunch of overseer types with heavy wooden shovels came running towards us.

We dumped the boat as far from them as we could and as close as possible to the tower. At the shore, while I was helping Brexxie and Bill off the boat, one of them clobbered me from behind with something thick, heavy, and hard.

I saw stars blinking in the firmament of my own visual field, then everything went dark.

10

The Ziggurat

I came to gradually, with a fine feeling of waking up gently in my own bed back in Long Island in the 21st century. Firm pillow under my head, warm Polo Ralph Lauren PJs covering my body, Egyptian cotton sheets over all.

Then my senses clicked in and I realized I was lying on cold, sun-dried mud bricks and everything around me smelled like an outhouse. And I realized all four limbs were stretched out as far as they could go, bound at each corner of the slab by flaxen rope or some kind of woven cloth. I opened my eyes and found myself staring into the blue sky above, noting the clear air and billowing white clouds. Thankfully the sun was going down and not directly overhead.

I heard a moan which sounded like Bill's voice and twisted my head in that direction. He was tied to a pole by his hands overhead, and his body sagged limply. Brexxie sat at his feet, tied with his hands behind him and leaning, eyes shut, against the upright log. No sign of his mitts, prod, or time boomerang.

I scanned visually in every direction I could see. As I feared, we were on top of the unfinished ziggurat, and it appeared I would be their next human sacrifice, as I was already tied to the altar. I guessed they planned to let the other two watch and then have their turns next.

I could see someone I took to be their high priest ready-ing himself for the sacrifice. He had long flowing robes on and stood with his back to me at a table behind the alter, on which stood a large basin of what I guessed had to be water. He seemed to be cleaning or consecrating a large dagger, with a sharpened flint blade and a handle encrust-ed with jewels. From what little of his skin I could see, mostly his hands and forearms as he handled the dagger in a ceremonial fashion, he seemed quite different from all the rest of the people here. Whereas they were dirty and hairy, he seemed clean, healthy, and almost glowing.

I struggled against my bounds, but they felt quite tight and unyielding.

A Ubaidian with a spear stood guard nearby and no-ticed my thrashing about. He yelled out, "Grug! Macblg!" Or at least that was how it sounded to me, but it was clear what he meant regardless of the words used.

Several more guards came rushing to the top of the structure, and one of them started slapping me about the head and face with an open palm. I guessed he wasn't one of my fans. Perhaps I had killed one of his relatives or friends during the melee onboard the yacht, and he was ea-ger for revenge.

Somehow shouted "Nid!" and he stopped.

In moments, the one Brex had earlier identified as Gen-eral Bnindagun approached, a linen bandage across his forehead. *He survived my strike when I defended against his axe swing, and I'll bet he wants revenge, too.*

Bill still sagged with eyes closed, but Brexxie was com-ing to and eyed the general cautiously.

From about twenty feet away, the general looked crossly at Brex and mimicked their previous encounter by holding his hands in the air as if choking an invisible throat but then shrinking back as an invisible window closed around his arms. Then he abruptly thrust his right hand in the air, fingers extended in what must have been the early Ubaidian equivalent to a Bronx salute.

Brex shouted at him. "Glid por okum! Brd!"

At that the general's head jerked back in surprise. He paused to consider, then answered back in a reasoned tone, "Brg natum. Brg, susnin!" And he pointed at his own chest.

Brex looked alarmed. "Nid! Nid!"

The war chief waved both hands horizontally, as if to negate what Brexxie just said. "Brg buh nid mrp." Then he pointed at his own chest again with a thick, hairy thumb.

Brex nodded reluctantly.

The general grunted and swirled his hand in the air towards his half dozen men nearby. One immediately cut loose my bindings, while another freed Bill, and he collapsed, apparently still out. A third released Brex, and he stood up, gingerly massaging his reddened wrists.

I wasn't sure whether to get up yet or remain lying on my back. I didn't want to interrupt whatever Brex was working on.

The guards backed off and re-assembled in protective positions around their leader, all except one warrior. That one received an order from the general and rushed off, leaping down the stairs of the ziggurat as fast as possible.

Brex eased over close to me. "Good news."

"I'll say. I thought they were going to sacrifice me first and then you two guys."

"That's exactly what they were planning to do. They just wanted us all three to be fully awake so we could appreciate every nuance of their ceremony. They didn't want any of us to miss a thing."

"How did you talk them into releasing us?"

"I didn't. And they're not. We're just unbound... for now, at least."

"How did you pull that one off, Brex?"

"I challenged him to a sort of duel. Trial by combat."

"Gosh, Brex, that was awfully brave of you." I sat up and realized my mitts were gone, too, and there was no sign of any of our weapons. But there was plenty of blood on the slab where I was laying before and now sitting. And I didn't think it was all mine. My lacerations from the earlier fight seemed to have stopped bleeding and started to scab over. At least the ones I could see.

"Not really," said Brex.

I eyed his opponent. "I disagree, Brex. He's got at least a hundred pounds on you and they are all muscle. How is that not brave?"

"Because I'm not doing the fighting. I told him that you were the strongest man and fiercest warrior where we came from and that *you* were challenging him in a battle to the death."

The full import of that began to sink in. "So you volunteered *me* to fight."

"Yes, I did."

"Thanks a lot, Brex."

"Look at it this way, my dear Jacks. If I didn't, we would all be dead within the hour anyway, slaughtered as sacrifices to their god Enki. But this way we have a chance."

"So if I win, we all go free?"

"That was the deal. Yes."

"But if I lose, we all die?"

"Most assuredly."

I looked at my opponent again. "I think I can take him. I'm not sure how they fight down here, so he may have a few tricks I'm not familiar with, but we are both about the same age and I think I'm a little bigger and stronger."

I could hear the noise of unseen people ascending the steps toward us, so many heavy footsteps that the bricks I sat upon began to quiver.

Brex said, "Sorry, buddy, but that's not how this works. He's the leader. If you are the strongest and best warrior from our place, you've got to fight the strongest and best warrior of this place."

"So he gets to pick the guy who fights me?"

"Yep."

"Well, based on those primitive spear shakers we saw on the yacht, I think I can take any one of those. Just one, right?"

"Yep. Their champion versus our champion. Mano a mano."

"Well, let's see which one of those little savages he picked!"

The noisy throng from below flooded the steps near the summit and began to chant like spectators at an international soccer playoff. The crowd parted, and the group on each side of the new path turned towards its center, whooping and hollering at their champion warrior as he ascended the steps towards the battlefield atop the ziggurat, the arena which would be the last ever seen by one of us.

Among the Ubaidians cheering and yelling, I could see warriors like those on the yacht, shore guards and overse-

ers as I had noted on land, and even the farmers and labor-
ers. For the first time since arriving in this time and place, I
could see also grown women—some old and decrepit, some
rather fetching in their furry animal-skin outfits—and some
older children. Here and there a young woman held a small
child or was clearly large and pregnant with one.

Out of the corner of my eye, I could see that Brexxie
had also noted the arrival of young women, and seemed to
have an interest. But the interest of the crowd clearly was
focused elsewhere. All heads turned towards a central figure who had to be mounting the stairs between them.

I kept struggling for a first glance at the man I had to
fight. Finally, I could see a thick head of hair, lush and
fuller than that of any of the others, rising from their midst.

I watched in awe as a mighty humanoid head the size of
a bull's came into view, then a thick and powerful torso as
massive as the slab I was seated on, then thick legs and
arms like enormous tree trunks. Unclad from the waist up,
his doubtlessly enormous privates were covered by a loin-
cloth made of mammoth hide, I thought.

This warrior made Goliath look like a kid in grammar
school.

"You mean *him*?"

Brex nodded.

"But he's got to be at least fifteen feet tall! That's not
even possible, is it?"

"You ever hear of the Giant of Castelnau?"

"Nope."

"In our day there have been many archaeological finds
of partial human skeletons, the bones of which were so
large that an extrapolation to a full skeleton would make it
as being in the range of twelve to fifteen feet tall."

"Come on, Goliath was only nine feet tall! I've never
even heard of any human taller than that."

"Well," said Brex, "in our time there have been many
reports of complete human skeletons in that twelve to fifteen foot range of height, but each has been found to be
simply mistaken identity, photoshopping as a prank, or an
outright scientific hoax."

"Brexxie, this man-mountain is not a hoax; he's very
much alive and real!"

"Ever hear of Andre the Giant?"

"The pro wrestler who used to be on TV and in the movies? He was over five hundred pounds of mostly muscle, but only about seven and a half feet tall. He couldn't even make the kid brother of this guy."

"True, but they may have had the same problem."

"Problem? *Problem*? Guys like this don't have problems, they make problems, they eliminate problems."

The crowd cheered as the giant turned around and around, thrusting his arms into the air and flexing his enormous muscles.

"No, dear Jacks. They have gigantism, an excess of growth hormone which causes bizarre and abnormal growth."

"But they're strong!"

"No, Jacks, they're weak. How do you think David killed his giant with only a sling and a pebble?"

"Thanks for the pep talk, Brexxie, but I don't see any weaknesses on this guy."

"I do."

"So you expect me to fight him?"

"That's up to you. But the general certainly expects you to."

I looked over and saw the general pointing at his hero, and the crowd cheered again and again. They shouted what must have been his name, but it sounded to me like 'Drmen.'

"So that's the bad news. You got any good news, buddy?"

"Sorry, Jacks, but that *is* the good news. You're not going to like the bad."

"I have a very, very strong feeling I won't. What is it?"

"I tried to talk the general out of it. You saw me argue with him. But he insisted. He said his way or nothing. I mean, he is the boss here, you see, so he's used to getting whatever he wants."

"So what does he want besides this living mountain of a hominid fighting me?"

"I tried to avoid this, Jacks, honestly I did."

"Avoid what?"

"The general insisted. He gets to pick the warrior and—"

"And what, Brexxie, my buddy, my pal, my dear friend?"

"—and he gets to pick the weapons and... and the animal."

"*Animal?*" I could feel the blood draining from my cheeks.

11

Fight to the Death

Brex peered off into space, as if trying to find some way to reassure me. "Don't panic yet. I know from studying world history what kinds of animals lived in this region and in this time."

"What kinds?"

"Red foxes, eagles, grey wolves, wild boar, vultures, gazelles, leopards, lions. In some places, brown bears."

"So pretty much everything but elephants and werewolves?"

"Yeah, I guess that's about it. And no rhinos either."

"But lions and tigers and bears—"

"Oh, my!" said Brex.

Bnindagun grunted something or other and all his folks backed off, took one step down the sides of the ziggurat, and completely encircled us.

The monstrous living mountain of a man now stood on top with the rest of us.

Bill Higgins finally began to squirm and moan and open his eyes. He looked at the two of us, the sacrificial altar covered in blood, the blue sky above, the Euphrates River in the distance, the warriors surrounding us on all sides, and the biggest figure he had probably ever seen, second only to the Statue of Liberty back home. "This is still a nightmare, right?"

"Sorry, bud," said Brex, "but it's not."

"You mean I'm really here, next to a living, breathing Wonder of the World, the Colossus of Rhodes?"

"'Fraid so, dude," said Brexxie helpfully. "But we'll get you home as soon as we can."

"But how? We're in the middle of some kind of time warp and about to get eaten by a crazed giant or something! Even our Hercules Jack is like a shrimp compared to this monster!"

"Try not to worry, dude," I said. "It's just when everything seems completely hopeless that our good friend Breslin Herndon, *agent extraordinaire*, can usually come up with something."

"You mean we still have a chance?"

"With Brexxie on our side, there is always a chance," I reassured him.

"Go back to sleep, bub," Brexxie said. "I don't think you want to witness what is going to happen next."

The nightmare giant in front of me growled as three underlings handed him a double-bladed axe the size of a Cadillac. *Three. It took three grown men about my size just to pick up that axe. It must weigh at least five or six hundred pounds.*

Then another warrior brought up a huge, clucking ostrich.

"Okay," said Bill, closing his eyes and rolling over.

The ostrich took one look at me and squawked in anger, as if I were trying to steal his mate.

I looked askance at Brex.

He raised his eyebrows. "Oh, yeah, I forgot about ostriches. They had them, too. Arabian ostriches were hunted to extinction only in the past century or so... of our time, that is. Watch out, they can kick you from here to Kalamazoo. Their legs are stronger than warhorses and farming mules. Stay clear."

"That's a nasty looking beak there, too."

"Oh, yeah, stay away from that, too."

"I don't suppose ostriches have any particular weaknesses like giants do?"

"Naw. Except for high-powered rifles. Hunting them was the sport of kings in this region for centuries, but they still thrived until the invention of high-powered hunting rifles."

"But I don't have a high-powered hunting rifle."

"Hmm, no, I suppose not. But you've got me and my lucky ring here." He took a ring off his thumb that I hadn't noticed before and placed in on my pinky finger. The large gemstone had a soft blue glow in the waning light.

"Don't I get an animal on my side, too?" I asked.

"We didn't discuss the details of that part. I think theoretically the animal is an independent player added to the mix to make the contest more exciting. Theoretically he could attack either of you."

"Theoretically, huh? That's comforting. I'll bet *this* ostrich plays favorites. He's probably trained with these guys before."

It would be dark soon, so other warriors lit several giant urns of oil, one on each corner of the temple top where we stood.

"Just remember, you've had more training than both these opponents put together. It's not just the size and strength of the warrior, but the skill."

"So, I've got to fight the biggest humanoid creature in the history of the world, the size of our mythical Paul Bunyan at least, a battleaxe as big as the average car back home, and a cackling, flightless bird who can kick worse than the strongest football player in America?"

"That's about the size of it, dear Jacks, it is."

"Aren't you glad right now that you are too tiny to fit into Bnindagun's plans?"

"Well, yeah, but I do have a big brain."

"And what good is that to me now?"

"When the time comes, you'll find out."

"So we're still in this together despite me facing obvious and certain death?"

"Have I ever let you down before?"

"Never."

"Well, I'm not about to start now. General Bnindagun isn't even playing checkers. He's playing whack-a-mole, but I'm playing four-dimensional Zantu chess."

"Cool."

"Just do your part... and I'll do mine. Trust me, buddy."

"I always do, Brexxie. I always do."

As I stood up, the mega-giant took a few practice swings, the gargantuan axe creating a cool breeze as it sliced through the air.

The general snapped his fingers, and another warrior bent over and slid his own battleaxe, the normal human size, along the brick surface towards me. I picked it up and admired the balance and feel. A fine though primitive weapon. But it was the size of a toothpick compared to that giant's baseball bat.

He stopped swinging, threw his head back in a raucous laugh, then howled at the moon, clenching his fists and arms, his deltoid and pectoral muscles swelling like inner tubes, but far more thick, solid, and powerful.

So, werewolves, too. This day just keeps getting better.

I tentatively swung my axe. Nice construction. I could get used to a weapon like this. If I lived long enough, that is.

The giant's huge, misshapen head then pointed directly at me and he roared defiance, emitting a wind strong enough to send clouds of dust off the bricks into my face, a wind reeking of raw boar meat and decayed teeth, each the size of my open palm.

I noticed his left eye projected a fierce, unholy gaze, but his right eye seemed unfocused, rheumy, and discoordinated.

He's got some kind of disease with impaired vision in that right eye... or maybe an old battle injury.

That face would haunt my dreams forever, but at that moment I suddenly felt calm, as if everything around me were surreal and I was just watching it on celluloid happening to someone else. Just sitting in the dark theater with my sweet babe Momma Sara, one arm around her, my heart feeling pure and at peace, munching on bright buttery popcorn with a tang of salt and guzzling down frizzy cola with a lot of cooling ice. A lot of cooling ice. Just me and the missus, enjoying a great movie, watching Tarzan on the screen deal with the heat and jungle and angry natives and fierce beasts. Yeah, just a movie. I felt calm, as if nothing could actually go wrong.

Until it did.

Moving faster than I thought a mountain could, my nemesis raised his mighty axe high overhead, high as the top of the temple pillars, and rushed me with such heavy steps the whole ziggurat shook. He flung down the axe in a rush of air straight for my head.

I dove and somersaulted and evaded the blow as it came down on the bloody alter with the sound of exploding dynamite, splitting the alter in half and sending up clouds of dried brick chunks and dust.

The ostrich had clucked and moved out of the giant's path, then zig-zagged from behind him towards me, but then was hit full in the face by the explosion of dust. Temporarily blinded, it screeched and hopped about in circles, kicking and scratching backwards like a cat burying his business in the litter box, furry eyelids blinking furiously.

I came out of my somersault low to the surface and missed the exploding cloud. I kept rolling away from it until nearly at the edge of the drop over the side.

Three warriors standing in a row there saw my approach and angrily denounced me in words I could not understand. One pointed back towards the fight, two others aimed their spears at my head, and all three began to kick at me when I rolled close enough.

I understood all that... but looking at their twisted and torn feet, I couldn't understand why podiatry took so long to emerge as a field. Any podiatrist in this tribe would soon own every nugget of gold for miles around.

Then I leapt up, raised my axe, and surged towards the bird.

Still blinking like mad, his view of me obviously indistinct, he nevertheless charged me and poked his hard beak towards my head. I ducked and swung my axe laterally towards his neck. He pulled back just in time and knocked me to the surface with his wing. I rolled over and over, trying to get away from his stamping feet as he charged.

By this time the giant was trying to get back into the action, pulling at the stuck axe to loosen it and backing up several steps.

The bird stomped on my legs with the two large toes of one foot as the giant bumped into him and sent him sprawling backwards.

Before the bird could recover, I leapt to my feet, swung the axe with all my force, and sliced the squawking head right off that muscular rope of a neck. The dying head fell to the surface with a surprised look in its grit-filled eyes. The body kept running in circles like a chicken with its head cut off, but then finally stopped and stood still for a moment, lost its balance, and toppled to the dusty surface.

The giant let go of his axe, its sharply honed stone head still stuck several feet deep into the altar. A look of grief on his face, the giant ran to the bird, picked up both pieces, and tried helplessly to meld them back together, yelling at the sky until teardrops the size of marbles formed and rolled down his cheeks.

"Good one, Jacks! Bravo!" yelled Brex from over by the pillar where Bill still lay crumpled and motionless. "You're doing better than I expected. Knight to rook. Next, knight to bishop, and then check the king. One down, two to go."

Panting, I realized my eyes were filled with dust now, too. "I thought you were going to help!"

"I am helping! I'm analyzing your opponent's moves to develop the appropriate strategy."

"Please let me know when you've finished."

"I will, Jacks, I will. Just give me a little more time."

"I'll give you all the time you want, but I'm not sure *he* will!"

The giant laid the bird pieces gently on the surface, bent low, and roared at me again. He seemed twice as full of rage now. Before he was fighting under orders. Now it was personal. The light in his left eye blazed like the fires of Hell.

But I noted again that the right eye appeared to be nearly useless.

The giant grabbed the handle of his axe and struggled to free it.

"I have it!" yelled Brexxie exultantly.

"Have what?" I stood there blinking, trying to wash my eyes clean from the settling cloud of dust.

"Remember how Andre the Giant died? And as a relatively young man of only forty-six. So strong, yet so weak."

"Before my time, Brex. No idea."

As the giant freed his axe and lifted it high overhead, I darted between his legs and slammed my axe as hard as I could into the Achilles tendon of his right ankle, then his left.

He roared in pain, dropped his axe, and reached with both hands behind him, trying to catch me with his hairy fists.

I scurried backwards as fast as I could to get away. He turned to chase me, but with both feet now bleeding, he was limping quite slowly, while I still remained nimble... at least for now.

"Heart failure, Jacks! Andre died of heart failure!"

"So? This guy's heart seems to be as strong as the 605-horsepower engine of a huge Mack truck!"

"No, it's not. I can see his chest quivering from here!" yelled Brex. "No humanoid can grow as big as Andre or this fellow here without suffering gigantism, overgrowth caused by an excess of growth hormone by the pituitary gland in the midsection of the brain, near the ventral surface, below the hypothalamus."

"Why don't you draw me an anatomical map, Brex, so I can see it better?"

"Later. No time now, my friend. But here's the point—unnatural overgrowth screws everything up. He's big and muscular but his heart is structurally flawed."

"Thanks for the anatomy lesson, professor." I struggled to leap between the giant's legs, hoping he would twist suddenly, lose his balance, and maybe fall and hit his enormous head on a corner of the altar. "He looks pretty strong to me!"

"No, Jacks, you're just looking at the outside. Look into his chest! He's got severe premature ventricular contractions, and I think I'm noting a bit of atrial fibrillation and the beginnings of asystole."

"Nice to see your diagnostic skills are intact, Brex, but what good does that do me now? Are you planning to send this guy to the cardiac unit at Einstein Medical Center?"

Pausing to glance at Brex, I failed to note in time that the giant had encircled me with both hands and was about to close in. Suddenly I was caught in a vise. He grunted in satisfaction, stood up tall, and brought me towards him for a closer look. I still clung to my axe, but both arms were clamped uselessly to my sides by the monstrous fingers, and I couldn't move.

He opened his mouth, and I noted again that greasy stench of raw boar bacon. I guess no one in this time knew about toothbrushes, decay-preventive dentifrices, and dental floss.

I started to gag. Maybe if I had a length of cable from the Golden Gate Bridge, I could at least give this guy's rotting teeth a good flossing before I died.

He opened wider and I realized he planned to bite my head off, in revenge for his ostrich pal losing his noggin.

Brex screamed out, "Jacks! The heart! Use my ring! The special ring!"

"Fine idea, Brex, but I can't move."

Not understanding our speech, at that moment the giant loosened his left hand grip, and the axe slipped from my numbed arms and landed on the surface below. He grabbed me with just his right hand as someone might pluck a cocktail sausage off a plate in order to plop it into his mouth.

My hands were free, and as I passed near his heart on my way to his gullet, I clamped the ring on his hairy chest. Even the hairs were thick and coarse like straws on a heavy broom, like thickets of briars in a forest.

The ring glowed blue and crackled with electricity, red surges that rippled through the surrounding sunburned skin and deep into his chest like bolts of pure lightning. For a moment, I could see through the rough, sunbaked skin and into the glowing red chambers of his heart, atria and ventricles alike, each as large as my fist, each pumping like the bilge pumps of the dying *Titanic* as it sank.

He roared in agony. But this time it was not the roar of rage and threat and confidence. It was the roar of a lion who has received a .458 caliber magnum bullet to the chest and senses it has only moments left before the savannah recedes into final darkness.

I karate-chopped straight into his one good eye. Left, right. Left, right. Left, right. The massive eyelid shut.

Then he let me go and clutched his left chest with both hands. I landed on the surface with a painful CLUMPFH, gasping in pain myself. I must have cracked at least one bone in my hand as I tried to cushion my fall.

The giant shut both eyes, moaned, and started searching for me by hand, a blind kid trying to find his little wild-caught pet, a lizard or turtle or baby robin, scraping, lunging, poking thither and yon, crawling on hands and knees as his ankles kept bleeding, his heartbeat growing more erratic, more irregular. More spasmodic.

Finally, thanks to Brexxie's lightning bolt ring illuminating it, I saw what Brex noted earlier, the irregular vibrations and undulations in the chest as the master bearer-of-blood within began to collapse, pulses and throbs of blood growing weaker.

The giant seemed to realize he was fading and emitted another terrible—but much weaker—roar, and then slapped and kicked all limbs in an effort to crush me into red paste.

I slithered towards the edge of the precipice, grabbing my axe along the way, mindful of the entranced natives frozen into place by what they were seeing.

The giant rose to a baby's crawl position, and I stayed on his right side, his blind side, and taunted him to come towards me.

"Yo, bully boy! Come and get me... if you can!"

He obliged and finally I saw my opportunity, his enormous carotid artery surging like a storm drain after a hurricane, sending gallons per second of blood into his feeble brain. I raised the axe as high as possible overhead and clapped down hard, like a 20-pound sledgehammer pulverizing concrete.

But with the honed edge of a primitive blade.

Right onto that pulsating vessel.

A huge spray of red blood emitted, like a fireplug after being suddenly opened by kids wishing to dance in the spray during hot summer heat. The giant rolled in the direction of my sound until he reached the edge of the temple tower and plunged over.

Dozens of screaming warriors and tribesmen on that side of the ziggurat scurried out of the way as the body tumbled over and over, down and down, some 100 feet or more to the dry red dust at the base. The vibrations of his mighty fall knocked over three of the oil basins at the top, and liquid flame spread all over the top in a tapestry of fluid colors on fire.

"Way to go, Jacks! We did it!" shouted Brex in jubilation.

"*We?*"

"Knight to bishop. Check king, then checkmate."

"I'm glad you know chess, Brexxie, but I don't, so I have no idea what you are going on about. And you could have simply told me his heart was about to crap out rather than yell all that medical mumbo jumbo."

As I looked down and saw flames slipping towards me on top of the bloody bricks, then peered over the edge and saw the Colossus of Rhodes at the base breathe its last, as I noted panic in the general and all his warriors, I suddenly felt very weak.

Very weak.

All my serum glucose was depleted.

I need some Peanut M&Ms.

12

The Sunken Ship

Brexxie grabbed Bill from New York, tried to slap him awake, and the two threaded their way through with the spreading flames licking at their heels. As the oil burned, a dark and greasy smoke filled the air with a stench like rancid boar fat. I could hear the sounds of departing footsteps and people screaming in panic, desperate now that their champion was gone.

At one point, some burning oil set Brex's chinos alight, but Bill helpfully bent over and patted out the flickering flames with his bare hands.

"Thanks," said Brex as they trod carefully towards the steps on the side facing the Euphrates.

"You'd do the same for me," muttered Bill.

Before they could take the first step down, the general, all his troops having fled, stood alone blocking their path. He grasped Brex around the neck as he had done earlier at Battery Park. He squeezed for all he was worth.

In an effort to help, Bill chopped at the choking arms, but to no avail. Brexxie's knees went limp and his legs hung uselessly as the general lifted him into the air and throttled the life out of him. Brex had no ethereal window to close on his opponent's hands now.

But I still had my axe and bounded to their side. "Move aside, Bill!" I exclaimed as I swung it at Bnindagun and missed.

Sensing the blade, he dropped Brex to the steps and leapt up to the burning top of the ziggurat. I bounded up after him, swinging my axe left and right again and again as he deftly bobbed out of the way of the swinging blade. He was smaller than the giant, far less powerful, but more clever and faster.

He reached within his linen tunic and produced a huge jeweled dagger, one with a sharp blade edge and extreme point. I backed off, mindful of the flames creeping around my feet, and waited for him to make the next move. I knew how I would face an opponent in my era, but I hadn't the slightest idea what a primitive savage might try.

In the end, he did make a primitive move, one that would prove to be his last. He emitted a shrieking war cry and charged at me head on, his leather sandals now on fire with burning oil.

I simply stood still, ready to swing my axe at the right moment, as he came into range. He raised his blade high and then struck straight down towards my chest. But before he could make contact, I swung the battle axe and sliced the general's head off in one mighty blow.

"Checkmate!" Bill yelled.

"You played a fine game of Zantu four-dimensional chess," said Brex.

The reek of burning blood and flesh filled my nostrils and I jogged towards the steps, my friends following.

"Thanks. But why did you keep calling this guy a general? That notion of a rank hierarchy seems completely unfamiliar in this place and time. He seemed to me more like a king, maybe, or a tribal chieftan." Oil and blood mingled on the top steps, and we had to be careful not to slip and fall as we started our descent.

"Right you are, Jacks, in this place and time. I was referring to the rank he will have in his modern day plot to conquer America in our place and time. Remember, I saw him at three different stages simultaneously in three facets of the Schimmerplotz window—our past, which is here right now, our present back home, and our future, which we as yet know nothing about."

"So you mean we'll see him again in his future, back in our present? How is that possible?"

With their champion and leader both gone, all the warriors and villagers seemed completely disorganized and incapable of challenging us as we neared the bottom. They scattered from our path, circling around us but never approaching.

"*How*, I can't explain. All I can tell you is that I saw it in the kaleidoscope of time which appeared as I prematurely slammed shut the Schimmerplotz in Battery Park. Maybe I triggered it accidentally."

"So in an alternate timeline of some kind, another version of the guy I just killed will still exist?" I stepped onto dry soil with a sense of relief, caring little about the chaotic cries and yells of people fleeing in all directions around us.

"At this point, that would be my best guess. Everything that would be normal in our timeline has been altered by someone or some force, perhaps from the future, coming here in this present and developing a vehicle for time travel."

Bill looked perplexed. "You mean we've been traveling in time? Why didn't you tell me that before you boarded my boat?"

Discarded weapons lay all about, and I noted the severed head of the general lying in the dust, eyes still open as if ready to take us on again. If Brex was right, he would... at least two more times.

Brex didn't even blush. "We can't control or even predict when a travel event will occur. But someone here can. The time-travelling subway from this primitive period to ours must be nearly complete. If we can't stop them, millions of these savages might penetrate to our time, too."

All the other natives were out of sight by now, either hiding in their huts or the more distant fields. But Bill spotted the villain's head and suddenly bounced up and down like a soccer player prepping for a game. Then he bent over, rushed the severed head, and kicked it for all he was worth.

I watched as the head sailed high and far, towards the darkening eastern sky as the sun set in the west, and the grotesque head landed beside the body of the giant.

"Score!" Bill shouted. "One zero. Game over."

Brexxie looked like Sigmund Freud pondering a peculiarly disturbed patient. "Soccer? I thought you said you were a professional lacrosse player!"

"I was... but that doesn't mean I couldn't play soccer, too. I'm a bit of a Manchester United fan. Always wanted to join the bros in roughing up the opposition team and their yokel supporters. Always wanted to kick some heads and tails."

I stood and watched, speechless, as he crowed and danced about and generally acted as if he had been on the field perpetrating the action rather than just watching from the sidelines. "Brex, time to get this guy home before he loses all of his ball bearings."

The soil grew moister as we approached the river.

"Agreed. Let's go do it, buddy. But say, did you note that cool chick eyeing me during your fight with the giant?"

"No, Brex. I was kinda busy at the time."

"You know, the one with the massive mammaries? She was about ten feet behind the general."

My shoes made slurpy sounds as the mud got deeper and slicker near the boats.

"Sorry, Brex, I guess I get a little absent-minded when I am fighting for my life."

"Anyway, she looked kind of hot. And interested. In me! Maybe I'd be better off living in a time like this where the cool chicks would think I was some kind of god or something."

Bill laughed, still sounding a bit off. "Yeah, Dr. Brains. I saw her, and she did seem interested in you."

I spied a boat with at least three paddles visible and headed for that. But the thought of Brex falling for some woman he knew nothing about vexed me. "I saw that movie, Brex. Not as great an idea as it sounds. One toothache in a time without dentists and you'd be longing for home. Celibate or not, it's better than rotting in this primitive, muddy sewer."

"Oh, heck, I guess you're right. Let's go back home."

"But where is your time boomerang?"

"It was right behind the altar. I just got it back. See?"

Mosquitoes were swarming again and I was eager to get moving. "Yeah, but the battery's dead, right?"

"So?"

"And the back-up batteries are on the sunken *Manhattan II* yacht."

"So?"

"Which was burnt to a crisp and now lies on the bottom of the most famous river in the history of the world, the Euphrates, which along with the Tigris delineated the land of Mesopotamia, and which with two other rivers marked the location of the Garden of Eden."

"So?"

"So? So? So how do we get dem batteries down dere, dum dum?"

"My dear Jacks, don't you realize you are talking to the smartest person in the world?"

They plopped into the boat. I shoved it towards deeper water and then sprang aboard. "So smart you left the batteries to sink when we fled the natives."

"But I still know where they are."

"You do?"

"But of course! I have a perfect cartographic memory!"

I guffawed at that. "Don't you mean perfect photographic memory?" I distributed the paddles and we rapidly headed towards deeper water.

"I have that, too. But I saw no reason to state the obvious. Cartography is a category subsumed by photography, so if I have the first, the second is implied automatically. It's just basic logic."

"Yeah... what you said."

Bill Higgins finally started to paddle. "I know what he means, dear Jacks. He has a mental map image of exactly where the boat went down. Global coordinates, degrees east and west, north and south, all that stuff."

I frowned. "Bill Higgins, I like you, and we have shared an important adventure together. Likely the biggest adventure in your life. But only Brexxie, AKA Breslin Herndon, can call me 'dear Jacks'. He and I have been together for a lifetime."

"Sorry, dude," muttered Bill. "No offense. I'm just all keyed up about our victories and the chance to go home! Just really wired. Never felt like this before."

In the middle of the river now, away from most of the mosquitoes, I paused, not sure where to head. "*Our?*" I paused and relented. *Everyone sees things only from his own perspective. Give the guy a break.* I turned to Brex. "So you have a mental image of where the sunken boat is. Now what?"

A fish jumped out of the water nearby and splashed down again.

"Well, admittedly, I may be off by a few yards. You have to factor in the size and weight of the boat, the volume of the run-off from all the tributaries and shore drainage into the river, the strength and speed of the current, and the friction with the river bottom, but I've got a pretty good idea where the yacht lies, give or take about sixteen point seven two inches."

"Inches? But isn't it deep? It's a river, for Pete's sake! One of the greatest rivers in world history! How are we going to get to the bottom and retrieve it?"

"*We?* Dear Jacks, I'll tell you where it is, but you are the only one capable of reaching it and retrieving all our valuables."

"That's what I figured." I was starting to sweat again from all the heat and humidity. Birds, or perhaps bats, were swooping around.

"Remember, I'm Dr. Brains and you are Mr. Brawn."

Bill guffawed. "And I played professional lacrosse for one season before I hurt my ulnar nerve and had to quit... but I was still a big hit with the ladies on the 'round Manhattan yacht circuit!"

"Good to know, Bill, thanks." I continued to humor him. *He's still in shock.*

Brexxie laughed.

Something flew close by me and I could see it more clearly. It was a bat, probably hunting the insects around our boat. "Brex, you expect me to descend to the depths of the Euphrates River—in primitive times, no less—and retrieve the devices which will allow us to return home?"

"Of course, my dear Jacks. I know you don't want to remain here. Not without Momma Sara and Little Sara and BigBear, am I right?"

Brex was certainly right about that! I would risk anything at this point to get home. But I needed to know what the risks were. "So how deep is this river, anyway? Two, maybe three hundred feet deep? Maybe a thousand? I'm supposed to hold my breath for seventeen or eighteen minutes and search through a sunken ship in utter darkness with my eyes closed?"

Brexxie laughed. "You've seen too many *Titanic* movies or something. This isn't the Pacific Ocean or Atlantic Ocean or anything remotely quite so deep as that. It's just a river, for Pete's sake."

"Just a river?"

"Yeah, the Euphrates River... about five hundred feet wide at its most narrow in this region, in Ubaidian days, and perhaps three times wider at its broadest. Maybe a mile and a half wide in a couple of key places. But, by golly, Jacks, in many places it was only twenty to forty feet deep. That's why the natives who have been trying to kill us for the past twenty-four hours were sitting in shallow river boats. Why do you think they were working with boats having a very shallow draft? Don't you notice the environmental cues around you which reveal everything going on in the background?"

I ignored the insult. "Twenty feet deep?"

"Yes."

I looked at the dark water. "I can dive that deep without even really holding my breath."

"I knew you could. In fact, even if the bottom of the boat is at forty feet, the area you'll search will still only be about twenty feet from the surface."

"But how do I see down there to retrieve our most important batteries to return us to our modern day?"

"No problem, buddy boy. I've thought of everything." Brex opened his Gant Brothers scarlet shirt and revealed a chest somewhat thicker than I ever remembered when we were kids swimming in the Bogue Falaya State Park in Louisiana.

Brex ripped open a zipper in what appeared to be his belly, but on closer inspection proved to be a flesh-colored wrap containing items secreted long before we started this mission. That was probably where his lucky electromagnetic pulse ring emerged from earlier. "Don't worry, buddy, I have flashlights here which will turn dark river water into bright noon-day sun." He pulled two out, each of which had a wrist band so I could carry them without having to grip them.

I shook my head. "Okay, you've got two bases covered. I can hold my breath and have light, but what about ferocious river monsters? What kind of wildlife might I encounter down there? Alligators, crocodiles, sharks, electric eels?"

"Nah, Jacks. Shouldn't be much worse that catfish, spiny eels, and giant turtles."

"*Shouldn't* be? But what if there is?"

He reached within and pulled out a stun gun, which I stuck in my waistband just as the sun was setting with a faint red glow above. Then Bill and Brex helped me paddle to where we had started a few hours before.

"A little more to the right, guys," said Brex, exercising his cartographic memory.

I tried one of the flashlights, and it turned night into day over ancient Mesopotamia, its brilliant arc reminding me of the World War II searchlights in London trying to help detect the incoming Nazi buzz bombs and V-2 rockets.

All three of us paddled 'til Brexxie called a halt. "Okay, here's the exact spot where we were when we left the boat."

I peeked around and it all looked just like muddy water to me. I couldn't get much of a sense of the surrounding landmarks or stars or rising moon to help me distinguish one spot from the next.

"Now I've got to figure how far she may have drifted downstream prior to reaching the bottom, and then how far she dragged along the mud after that."

"Go right ahead."

He pointed downstream. "Go about ten more yards this way."

We did.

"Now stop. Oh, wait, I forgot to figure in the reduced profile of the yacht as it burned. Most of the superstructure was destroyed, so with a reduced profile to catch the current it would have drifted less. Go back about twelve yards."

We did.

Brex turned to me. "My briefcase should still be under the table where we were wining and dining thanks to our dear friend Bill Higgins here."

Bill smiled and patted Brex on the back.

Brex gave him a thumbs-up. "If it got settled in the cracks somewhere and you can't get the whole case, just open it and grab the batteries."

"What do they look like?"

"Just like regular laptop power packs. Only much smaller. The goal is to maximize power but minimize bulk size and weight, you see."

I stood up, taking several deep breaths and preparing to dive.

"Oh, two more things. If you have to open the case, mind the booby trap."

"Sure, like I've got nothing better to do than figure out how your booby trap works while I'm relaxing down there."

"Jacks, with your limited intellect you'll never figure out *how* it works. That's not the point. Just don't trigger it. I gave you a normal case before we left home, but if you try to open mine normally, it will explode with knockout gas right in your face. You have to ignore the front of the case and open it on the back side, where it looks hinged but isn't. Push both back corners at the same time, and it will open from what seems to be the back."

"Got it." I kicked high into the air so that I could arc up and plunge down as I drew my final huge breath of fresh air before entering the dark water.

"Wait!" screamed Brex. "The other thing. I just remembered the other kind of river animal around here."

I could hardly pause in the middle of a dive once I initiated one.

As I plunged into the cold brown liquid, I thought I heard his final word. "Snakes!"

Thanks to Brexxie's brilliant lights, I espied the burnt-out hulk of the *Manhattan II* in no time. Most of the framework holding the glass panels was gone, and huge glass sheets and broken shards littered the area in and around the boat. Part of the frame still stood, with the occasional intact but smoked-up panel still in position, but more commonly holding sharp, irregular, and jagged shards of glass.

What disturbed me most, however, were all the dead and bloodied bodies of the slain warriors we'd left behind. Nothing quite like death and dead bodies to focus the mind. Most days you just wander through life, rushing from one exacting detail and minor crisis to the next, never stopping to smell the petunias, and then suddenly you are old and running out of time.

Seeing dead bodies makes you feel morbid. Old and frail. Mortal and temporal. I don't recommend it, but if you've ever been in combat, you know what I mean. If you haven't, then don't belittle folks who have been there and seen it all and then developed PTSD later.

Just thank your lucky clovers that you haven't experienced it yet yourself. It ain't pretty and you won't ever be the same again once it has happened.

In this cold, dank water, although it had probably been 30 to 40 seconds since my last breath, I could hold on easily for at least two minutes.

The blood had attracted a wide variety of hungry waterlife, everything from small minnows through mid-sized carp about the size of my open hand, to quite large catfish and game fish like mangar, all the way to the eels Brex had mentioned.

Then I saw it... and the other it.

The first it, the table where we had sat, was scorched but largely intact. I could see the briefcases clearly in the area near where our feet had been. Mine was wide open, various contents all spilled out. In my haste to retrieve the mitts and time prod, I must not have re-closed it properly. But there sat Brex's also, still intact, the one which held our only possible chance of returning to our place and time. No way the local natives would let us sneak into their time travel device.

But then I saw the other *it*, a water snake gnawing on the remains of one of the Ubaidians.

And it was big.

Very big.

Coiled up enjoying dinner no more than a few feet from the essential briefcase.

I was running out of air now, so ascended straight up for a fresh breath. The sky above was completely dark now, but with my right hand I pointed the light around until I located the boat holding my friends, no more than 20 feet away.

While treading water I yelled out, "Found the wreck, guys. You guessed it right, Brex!"

"Guessed? Guessed? I never *guess*, my dear Jacks. I calculate; I make informed calculations."

"Whatever. But you forgot to warn me about the giant snakes. There's one about the size of an anaconda down there munching on one of the dead warriors right next to your briefcase."

"Oh, you mean a Hedammu! Don't worry, Jacks, that's just an old Mesopotamian myth. No such fossil or skeleton from this region has ever been discovered in our time."

"Myth? Fossil? I'm telling you it's alive and it's down there right now!"

"Relax, Jacks. Even if you aren't just imagining it, that stun gun should handle it. It could stop anything up to the size of a large shark or alligator gar."

"Sharks? There's sharks, too?"

"No, Jacks. Freshwater, remember? I just used that as an example of size."

I exhaled in disgust, took a deep breath, and plunged back down.

I must have moved too quickly or at too sharp an angle. When I got about halfway down, the stun gun slipped loose from my waist and plunged down into the muddy area beyond the edge of the ruined yacht.

And the Hedammu didn't want to wait while I looked for it. Tired of gorging on old, cold dinner, he headed towards fresh meat—me. I was about five feet from the briefcase when he wrapped his tail around my legs and abruptly jerked me out of reach of it. I twisted and thrashed but couldn't get loose.

Then he opened his giant maw, large enough to snap off my head in one bite. *What is it with stuff in this time period wanting to bite off my head?*

I tried to kick up towards the surface, but he held my legs tight, like a bucket of cement employed by the mob back home to silence a rat once and for all.

As my hands flailed about, the lights jerked around randomly, making parts of him suddenly visible in the middle of the midnight dark as that primeval mouth threatened to eat me alive. One second I could see nothing but water with minnows scurrying away in the distance, then suddenly I could see sharp teeth the size of my fingers, still wrapped in Ubaidian gore, lunging straight at my face. As the head darted forwards, just a couple of feet away now, I clapped my hands together right in front of his face, trying to blind him.

He turned away from the combined power of two ultra-bright lights and loosened his hold on my legs just long enough for me to reach the briefcase, and I grabbed its handle. I was running out of air again, but luckily the brief-case came loose from beneath the burned seat.

Before I could kick off for the surface, the Hedammu turned to attack me again, this time closing its eyes and ramming towards my midsection with a wide open mouth, bloody jaws agape.

I grabbed the rear of the case, pointed the front edge towards him, and reached for the snaps on front. Just as he was about to close in, I released the snaps and with a sharp popping sound, gas gurgled out like a giant whale fart, exploding directly into his startled face.

Still holding the case from the safe edge, I thrashed to the surface and exhaled just before I passed out, then breathed in the most wonderful infusion of oxygen since probably my first live breath after birth 35 years ago.

With my light from my right wrist on him, I could see Brex smiling. "Get it, Jacks?"

Treading water with legs and one arm, I raised the case with my left hand, sending a searchlight bright into the night sky towards a new Ubaidian moon 8,000 years ago.

"Great! That's my Jacks! Get me the batteries and let's go home."

"Say, Brexxie," I mused as he took the case and Bill helped me over the side of the boat, "do you think we should take that Hedammu carcass with us so all the ar-cheologists, paleontologists, and anthropologists of our day can get the story straight, that it's for real and not a myth?"

"Jacks, I think you are lightheaded from the lack of ox-ygen. There's not a scratch on you beyond those scabbed-over ones from our earlier struggles. I'm telling you it is just an old Mesopotamian myth. All the scientists of our day know that."

"Not a scratch? What do you call this gash on my fore-arm?" I showed it to him.

"Sorry. At least he didn't get to eat you. My stun gun took care of him, right?"

I thought about my carelessness in losing the gun. "Yeah... right..."

"Well, there you go, then. One dead Hedammu; one live Agent Jack Rigalto."

As Brex retrieved the batteries, I lay on the boat, my chest still heaving. "You have no interest in proving all our modern scientists wrong and correcting the record?"

Brex laughed. "I do that every day as it is. I don't need another feather in my goose-down pillow, and it won't really matter in the modern world anyway, will it?"

I shrugged.

"I think we've got bigger issues to deal with right now, like—"

"I'm wet and cold," I broke in. "Let's just get back to the present and do what we can to defend our future."

"Sounds good." Brex fiddled with the batteries and snapped a switch, which made his device hum and glow softly in the darkness. "You first, Bill."

"I'm game. Sounds good to me."

"Now, I don't have one of those sci-fi memory erasers, so you'll remember whatever you experienced on this trip."

"You bet I will. 'Til the day I die. And I'll never forget what you guys did for me. I owe you my life." His voice grew soft and began to crack.

I shifted the lights so none illuminated his face.

Brex put the device in position. "But you realize what will happen to you in our day and age if you start blurting out the truth?"

"No. What?"

"Half the people will think you are lying and hate or despise you. The other half will know you are crazy and want to lock you up."

"But it's the truth! Why such consequences?"

My chest had stopped heaving, and I could breathe normally now. "Bill, if you yap about all this, all the girls back home will think you are nuts and avoid you like an STD. You'll never get a date again."

His eyes bulged and he gulped. "I won't say a word. Not a peep out of me. Nothing. I swear."

13

The Return

Bill went first. One moment he was there on the Ubaidian boat with us on the river, and the next moment he was gone. The dark water still lapped at the sides of the boat, which plopped up several inches as Bill's weight vanished.

"You next, old buddy," Brex said to me.

"Do you reckon it hurts?"

"Not as far as I can tell. It seems to hurt no more than being carried into, through, and out a dark tunnel by train."

"Okay. Thanks." I looked back one last time towards the ziggurat, its grandiose shape still visible in the flickering flames of light on its top, almost like some kind of lighthouse.

"Since when are you worried about pain anyway, Mr. Tough Guy? I've seen you laugh at pain. I've seen you get creamed on the football field, sustain a broken leg, then as the stretcher bearers cart you off, you smile at your cheering fans and wave and give them high-fives."

"This is different. I know I'm about to do something which seems full of risk. If I had gone into that LSU versus Tulane game knowing I'd break my leg, it likely would have felt ten times worse." With the adrenaline from my fight with the Hedammu wearing off, at that moment I was starting to notice the pain of my various wounds, and the swelling in my hand that broke my fall from the giant's grasp. That hand throbbed.

"Imagine a hundred times worse," said Brex. "With my hypersensitive, fast-responding neurons, any irritant minor to you is magnified a hundredfold for me. Imagine you hear a tiny child's drum with a light tap, tap, tap with a little plastic drumstick. In the same situation, I'll hear a brass band with the huge bass drum going BOOM, BOOM, BOOM right in my ear."

"But there's got to be an upside to all that sensitivity, right, Brexxie? A rose smells that much sweeter, a Peanut M&M tastes that much more divine, a tender kiss totally enrapturing and enthralling." The thought of food made me realize how hungry I was getting. I needed dry clothes, a couple of beers, and a thick cheeseburger cooked rare, plus some TLC from my beloved wife.

Brex smiled 'til I reached that third example. Then he looked sour with psychic pain, the many times he'd been deprived what he longed for. "You know no girl has ever kissed me, Jacks. Low blow."

"I'm sorry, Brex, I didn't mean it like that. I was just remembering things in my life which give me pleasure and then imagining how a more sensitive nervous system could heighten the experience. I didn't mean to touch on a sore spot. Forgive me?" I shivered involuntarily. The day's intense heat was giving way to night chills, especially considering how wet I was.

"I could never stay mad at you, Jacks, if I were even capable of getting mad in the first place. And I'm not capable. My aloofness makes me so distant at times that I deal with things like that purely in the abstract, with no emotions triggered. I'm nearly incapable of being angered or getting mad."

I nodded. "So that's your secret."

"Do you want to sit here and keep talking in the dark or get on home?"

"Sounding a little mad there, buddy."

"Don't push me, Jacks. My neuronal glucose is approaching all-time lows. Now put your girl-kissing hands on this boomerang and hold still."

A strong wind blew over us, and I realized a storm had to be approaching. I could imagine, but not see, billowing clouds moving in overhead. I reached out and gripped both ends of the loop while he fiddled with controls in the middle. "Wait. Brex?"

"Yeah?"

"Is this a two-person operation? After me, can you use this on yourself, too?"

"I sure hope so. I don't want to stay in this place by myself. And now that they know we are here, they must be guarding the entrance to their time travel device, making that unusable although Sara and I escaped that way before. I think I can flip the final switch with my nose or a toe."

I shivered again as the boat began to rock with the gusts of wind. "I still don't understand how this even works. When you first disappeared with Little Sara in Battery Park, you came back without this time boomerang thingie. She said you went to the tower and jumped through something, and suddenly there you were. All the while, it appeared to me that you had never left and were still both just standing there in front of the Schimmerplotz."

"Sara was talking about the same ziggurat as on this trip, and the same general and group of warriors. But that first time, we stumbled onto their time train and used it to reach modern times, just as these Ubaidians are about to do."

The rocking increased and I was starting to feel nauseous. But I couldn't leave him there without *knowing* he'd be safe. "This trip we never had a chance to make it that far into the ziggurat. But between trips you fabricated this boomerang thingie. Is that a time machine?"

"Not really. I can't use it to go someplace in the past or future of my own choosing. I can only return home from whatever destination a Schimmerplotz takes me."

"I don't get it." A flock of unseen birds called overhead as they fled the advance of the coming storm.

"Think of it as a kind of time bungee cord. You tether one end on the middle of the Brooklyn Bridge and jump off. You can't just land any place in the world you like, but you can bounce right back towards where you started. You can crawl back up the cord to there."

"So you're talking about a kind of elastic time cable which can stretch through the space-time continuum?"

"My, I'm impressed! Hanging around me for so long seems finally to be rubbing off on you! I think you've actually learned something."

He'd be safe. Time for me to shut up, stop asking questions, and get home before we capsized or something. I shrugged off the jibe. "So the other end is tethered back home. Where?"

"In my secret lab, running through a conduit in the special briefcase on the yacht."

"Which is now in your lap here," I pointed out.

"Aw, just forget it. You'll see."

Brexxie flipped the switch and all in one instant the dark riverboat disappeared and instead I saw Manhattan's skyline in the middle of broad daylight, the UN complex, the *Manhattan II* yacht in the East River, and Bill Higgins rematerializing on the boat.

Then I found myself back on my original seat with my glass of Veuve Clicquot Champagne unfinished but still chilled, Bill standing at his position with his microphone, and Brex materializing in the center of the boat just a couple of feet away from his original seat. We left the Schimmerplotz increasingly behind as we plowed ahead on the East River and I watched without blinking until the shimmering window rapidly shrank following our exit and closed with a final ripple in the blue sky.

We had gone perhaps twenty yards in this space-time, while spending a day or so in the other one, and everything looked normal again here at home... except for the odd way the staff members all looked at each other, at me, and at Brexxie when he abruptly re-appeared at my side, still munching on a couple of Peanut M&Ms.

I turned to him, and he smiled. "Good to be home, isn't it, my friend?" he asked.

"Boy, have you got that right. But if we had died in that space-time, we would really have died, right?"

"I'm not completely sure. That is an empirical question which can only be answered by a controlled study which I don't want to risk initiating. But one thing I know for sure. The general's death back eight thousand years ago isn't permanent. Either that or there are multiple versions of him which will crop up again."

That was a problem for another time. For now I was happy. "Have another M&M, buddy," I muttered, still beaming.

Bill Higgins walked over and gave both of us a knowing wink. "Can I get you fellows anything else?"

I drained the rest of my Champagne. "I am still a bit thirsty!"

Bill snapped his fingers, and the cute girl at the bar sashayed over, still looking a bit confused. "Wanda, break out the special stuff that we usually save for the mayor and governor and VIP dignitaries from abroad."

"You mean the Dom Perignon Champagne and Beluga caviar and the Alaskan king crab legs?"

"Yeah, all of it. Give 'em everything we got. Nothing's too good for my new friends here."

"Yeah, I think I know what you mean. Coming right up!"

"Oh, and phone James at the pier and tell him to have a bucketload of Peanut M&Ms when we get back there. Okay, sweetie?"

"You got it."

Bill winked at us again, then back at the luscious young lovely and winked at her.

I supposed the adrenaline rush of their recent misadventure made them noticeably more affectionate. Either that or our joint experience made us seem more like friends than customers.

Maybe both.

After she stepped away, Bill sat at our table, leaned in conspiratorially, and whispered. "Come on, guys, is there anything else I can do for you? I mean anything. You wouldn't believe the connections I have made on this yacht over the past couple of years. I know just about everybody who is anybody in New York City, and several hundred folks from Albany and other places. You know, governors, mayors from across the U.S., not to mention foreign dignitaries from nearly all over the world."

I had a brainstorm. "I'll bet you know lots of the UN delegation folks."

"Of course I do! On average I'll host one of their groups every week."

"I just want to get kissed," muttered Brex with a morose look. "Jacks here won't let me date Aussie ladies too old for me or cave girls too uneducated."

Bill glanced at him then looked more closely at me. "I could fix you up with blind dates, no problem. I know lots of the theater directors and show girls and Rockettes and stuff, too. Interested?"

"Not me," I said. "I'm married. But maybe you could set Brex up with someone. I could bring my wife, you could bring Wanda, and we could do the town together one evening."

Bill eyed Brex again. "I know a few girls who might be interested in a Brainiac."

Brex suddenly looked as if he had won the Megabucks Lottery. "I have a great idea. Instead of doing the town, maybe you could get all six of us invited to one of those UN cocktail parties!"

14

Flash Mob

It took roughly three hours in normal New York time to circumnavigate Manhattan, but after all we had been through, it felt like days before we finally returned to Pier 62.

As we disembarked, the female bartender and waitress, the two crew Brex had saved first and sent home when the Ubaidian melee broke out on the yacht, smiled lavishly at him and escorted him off the deck. Once on the pier, each took one of his arms and they sashayed up the pier side by side all the way to the exit, cooing and thanking him without really mentioning what they were thanking him for.

Bill held back briefly to talk with me, handing me one of his business cards. "I made some calls from the boat. Everything's all set for the cocktail party tonight. All the details are on the back of my card. You three meet me in the parking lot at eight sharp so I can give you your official invitations and introduce Brex to his new date."

"Then we go into the Delegates Dining Room together?"

"Yeah, it's on the fourth floor of the UN Conference building and has one of the largest outdoor terraces in all of New York."

"Cool. So you and Wanda?"

He winked at me. "That depends on how this afternoon goes with her below deck."

"But at the UN party, the Canadian delegation will be there?"

"I can't promise that, but I expect so. I know they've been invited and delegates don't usually miss these things without a really good excuse."

"Thanks, Bill."

Just then a member of the shore crew came bounding down the pier from the ticket office. "Here's that bucket of Peanut M&Ms you asked for."

Bill nodded at me, and I took it. Must have been a hundred personal packs in there. The bucket looked like a homeowner's supply to hand out to all the neighborhood kids on Halloween. "Thanks, guys!" A huge bucket, but it wouldn't last long.

The girls left Brex as I joined him. He took one look at the bucket. "I think that is the most I've ever seen in one spot outside of a candy store!"

"Yeah. It's looking more and more like Bill Higgins is an awesome friend to have."

We left the port area and continued on the esplanade as it curved into Chelsea Riverside Park just to the north.

A shame Brex would never get to taste the huge bucket of fresh supplies of his favorite treat.

Suddenly a group of about 30 young toughs emerged from the bushes and the skatepark zone and surrounded us. In my mind I could see the coming headline for the crime incident report in the New York Times: "Bodies of Two Local Men Found in Chelsea Riverside Park." I could imagine cops knocking on our door in Long Island to tell Sara the news: "Our condolences for your loss."

Some of these guys had brass knucks, a couple had shanks, and several looked tough enough to be training for the Golden Gloves. All were taller than Brex, even the youngest, and nearly half were about as tall as me. Even if I could survive a bad beating with a concussion and a few broken bones, I wasn't so sure about Brex.

One particularly large guy separated from the circle and stepped forward. He eyed me cautiously, looked dismissively at Brex, then pointed at the bucket. "Guess we missed Halloween at your place, dude. Thanks for bringing the treats to us. Now hand it over."

"Not going to happen, my man," I said firmly. "Now you guys run along and get back to your skating or smelling the flowers or whatever else you were doing."

Nervously, Brex whispered, "Just give him the candy, dear Jacks. We can always get more later."

The ringleader snickered. "What the little weasel said, dear Jacks! Hand over the bucket... and your wallets, too." The whole group took a step closer, tightening the circle. Despite being in the open air by the waterside, I suddenly felt stiflingly hot.

I shook my head firmly.

The ringleader looked annoyed. "I've never seen a more mismatched pair in my life. One a regular Arnold Schwarzenegger and the other a little Arnold Pipsqueak. You think you two can handle thirty of us?"

I started swinging the bucket back and forth, very lightly, just a few inches. Then I took a slow step in his direction. Then two fast steps, halving the distance between us. "I was going to let you walk away free and clear before you pulled that one. But no one insults my best friend like that and walks away without making an apology."

The leader's facial expression changed from a mocking sneer to caution, but he didn't move.

I offered him a painless way out, one more time. "Are you going to apologize and walk away on your own two feet while you still can?"

The toughs in the crowd began to murmur among themselves. I could hear a few speaking in English, a handful in Spanish, and a bunch in a tongue which I couldn't make out at all.

The ringleader pulled his shank, held it high, and charged me.

I was only ten feet away and immediately swung the heavy metal bucket straight up into his chin. His head snapped back, the knife flew into the air, and he crumpled to the pavement like a burst balloon, blood oozing from both corners of his mouth.

As toughs yelled and milled about, some charging and others retreating, I caught the knife in midair as it descended and now had one weapon in each hand. Candy packs had flown out of the bucket as I swung it and rained down on the crowd, adding to their confusion. Some stopped to catch the candy as if it were a treat flung to them from a float at a Mardi Gras Parade. Some saw their crumpled leader on the pavement, turned, and ran while they could.

About a dozen made the biggest mistake of their lives.

They charged.

Our briefcases had disappeared in all the space-time shifts, but Brex still had his hidden weapons compartment in that torso belt. As I swung my weapons wildly, trying to knock assailants down with the bucket rather than slash them with the knife, he zipped himself open, reached within, and pulled out something. He pointed it at those who came near, pressed a button, and invariably they shrieked, turned and fled, screaming. The ones using English said, "I'm on fire! I'm burning up!"

With the bucket empty, four unconscious assailants on the ground, and the rest fleeing for their lives, I turned in amazement to Brexxie. "What the kaboodle was that, man? Did you kill them?"

"No, Jacks, don't be ridiculous. It's just the latest non-lethal weapon to break up crowds and mobs and violent demonstrations. I didn't even invent this one, though I did miniaturize it for hand use. It's in all the papers. Just a microwave pulse weapon to make people feel as if they are on fire, but it doesn't really harm them at all. Even the NYPD special units have this one. Geez, Jacks, don't you know anything?"

I stepped over to the ringleader and poked him with my foot to make sure he was really out. The bleeding from his mouth had stopped. I spat out, "And you don't get to call me dear Jacks. Not ever!" I turned back to Brexxie. "What was that odd language some of them were using?'

"You mean you haven't learned to recognize it yet after all we've been through?"

I peered at him in befuddlement.

He sighed. "I guess the general finished his time train and is now sending his troops through."

"You mean...?"

"Yep. Some of them were speaking Origanis with a Ubaidian accent."

"That sure doesn't explain how quickly they got integrated into local, modern gangs."

"Definitely not," Brex said solemnly. "This points to collusion with already established forces here in our current time, who have organized this whole thing."

"Could it be those UN guys you were talking about before?"

"I'm not sure, but that's our only lead so far."

15

Tara

Since all three of us adults were headed for the cocktail party at the UN that evening, we invited Auntie Tara to come over from Manhattan and stay with Little Sara and BigBear.

Even without the stress of working on a book, the two sisters bristled at each other as they criss-crossed paths in the house. Momma Sara wanted to look the best of her entire life for the most prestigious outing she had ever been on. Well, maybe second most. I think we both considered our wedding of ten years, two months, and seven days ago to be the most important social event of our lives. Her late parents had put everything they could afford into giving us a primo wedding at the Tchefuncta Country Club near Covington, an hour's drive north of New Orleans.

Not to say they'd had a lot to give. Her father had been a petroleum engineer prior to retiring, and most folks would consider them well-to-do. But that was because most folks in that region in those days were poor. Sara and Tara's family was solidly middle class, maybe at the upper end of middle class financially, but still middle class. She didn't attend a private academy and grow up with her own pony and riding lessons at a ritzy equestrian center, nor did she regularly take tennis lessons from the country club's pro.

Like me, she grew up attending public schools in Covington, learned to fish and hunt, and spent most of her time outdoors. Not that I paid much attention to her in those early years. She was two years younger than me, and just a scrawny, pre-pubescent sixth grader when I was a popular athlete in eighth grade, the final year of junior high, one of the stars in all the school sports.

I couldn't have had less interest in her in those days, when we first met. But puberty changed all that, as it does. By the time we were both in high school, she had blossomed and filled out very nicely, and suddenly I couldn't keep my eyes off her. We both did Junior ROTC together and came to realize how much we had in common. Like my best pal Brexxie, we realized we had the exact same value structure, believing in God, family, and country—in that order.

She and I both went to LSU in Baton Rouge, she majoring in English and I in food science. Not the best choice of major for the career I ended up in, but at the time it made sense. I liked everything to do with food, so found the studies quite interesting, but also not too taxing considering I spent several hours each day with football and every spare minute I could with Sara.

Brexxie earned his high school diploma halfway through freshman year, and I barely saw him for several years as he sailed through Tulane University in just two years with a triple major in physics, chemistry, and biology, then went to MIT and earned two doctorates, one in astrophysics and the other in biochemistry.

By the time Sara and I were freshmen at LSU and deeply in love, Breslin Herndon was the youngest Ph.D. professor at MIT in history.

And Tara? She was an identical twin, but the odd man out. She never quite got along with the other three of us, and now seemed a perfect time for her to get some minor psychological revenge.

As Sara rushed back and forth getting ready for the UN, Tara got up to her old tricks.

I was shaving in the bathroom, wearing nothing but underwear, when she snuck past Sara, crept up behind me, threw her arms around me, pressing herself into my back, and whispered huskily, "Hey, big boy, what say you and I skip the party and have a romantic evening for two instead?"

Unlike my usual polite brush-off, this time I didn't even pause as the triple floating heads of my Remington electric shaver rolled over my face. "Knock it off, Tara. We're going to be late."

"How do you always know it's me?" she protested, letting go but making eye contact with me via the mirror. "We're identical twins, for Pete's sake. We have all the same genes."

"There's more to life and personality than genes, sister-in-law. I could tell you apart from the first day I met you both as kids."

"But how? Our parents treated us both the same, gave us similar sounding names, and always dressed us alike. They did everything you *aren't* supposed to do with twins, and I sometimes hated them for it."

"That's one of the differences between you two right there. Given the same situation of fallible parents trying to do the best they knew how, Sara always focused on the aspect of them trying to do their best and loved them for it. You, on the other hand, focused rather on the fallibility aspect, their shortcomings, and resented them for it."

In the mirror, she looked steamed. And it wasn't because the mirror was steamed. I hadn't even showered yet. "You know, Jack Rigalto, sometimes you really tick me off!"

"That's another difference between you two. Sara has a lot more patience and doesn't go from hot to cold in two seconds flat."

She crossed her arms and furrowed her brows. "I'm beginning to wish I hadn't come over to babysit. I love Little Sara, but maybe I'd be better off if she came over to my place on the Upper East Side."

"You see, that's—"

She hissed, her eyes flashing, "Don't you dare explain any more differences between the two of us. I've had enough!" And with that, she flounced out of the room and bumped into sister Sara.

Startled, Sara muttered, "Excuse me!"

Tara kept storming out. "Little Sara, why don't we take BigBear for a walk while your parents get ready?"

"Yay!" exclaimed our little girl. BigBear barked and I could hear his paws thumping on the floor as he leapt off the furniture and scurried towards the front door.

Sara eased into the bathroom and looked at me in the mirror. "What was *that* all about?"

"Just Tara being Tara."

"Don't be too hard on her, me Jackie boy. She did drop all her plans at the last minute to help us out tonight. It wouldn't hurt if you showed her a little appreciation."

Suddenly I felt a twinge of guilt for being so cold and blunt.

Then Brexxie's voice at the door said, "Jacks, are you decent?"

"I usually am, but not always, it seems."

"I mean, may I come in? I have some big news."

"Of course, buddy. We're both dressed."

But Brexxie had emerged from his lab only half-dressed and in a state of distress. "Have you been monitoring the news?"

"No. Not since we got home."

"It's been happening all over."

I nodded to Sara and she got the hint, realizing we were going to talk business. She headed for the closet to select her shoes or something.

I turned to Brex. "*What's* been happening all over?"

"More of those feral wolfpack attacks such as we experienced at Chelsea Waterside Park a few hours ago."

"Where?"

"Various big cities all over the country. Large gangs of so-called youths, often thirty to fifty or more punks, suddenly forming and attacking everything in sight. Many stores have been looted and ruined, and lots of ordinary shoppers and pedestrians in the street have been savagely beaten, knocked down, and occasionally murdered."

"And you think there's a connection?"

"Well, of course there's a connection. Gangs don't suddenly sprout all by themselves like mushroom patches in the woods. The only question is *what* is the connection?"

"And who's behind it?"

"Yes," said Brex. "That, too, and also why?"

"But given what we've experienced over the past few days, you think rotten apples in otherwise good barrels of allied nations' UN delegations have something to do with Schimmerplotz space-time travel, General Bnindagun, and his Ubaidian hordes of barbarians?"

"That, my dear Jacks, is something I hope we'll be able to discern later this evening. And remember this—these bad apples are the ones that sent the Ice Man's hit squad after us the other day. Obviously they know who we are. So don't eat or drink anything they personally offer to you tonight."

"That's going to be tough for a hungry guy like me."

"Well, I'm bringing pocketfuls of Peanut M&Ms... you could do the same. Of if you do eat their food, take it from a tray open for all."

"That makes sense. I'll just avoid anything being offered specifically to me. And I'll warn Sara, too. Thanks, Brexxie."

16

Cocktail Party

Momma Sara looked lovely in her black Rachel Parcell long sleeve lace dress with ruffled accents around the skirt. In the chauffeured Lincoln Town Car which drove us to the party, she was excited and bubbly and unusually talkative.

I was happy to see her enthused, but there was something about the lacy, ruffly dress surrounding her rich, womanly form which really turned me on. I called it Rigalto's Law—the cuter the clothes Momma Sara wore, the more I wanted to see her with no clothes at all.

Brexxie was nearly mute, lost in thought. He kept consulting his smartphone, which he had designed himself, but didn't reveal to me at all what he was monitoring. We couldn't risk having Sara or the chauffer hear anything important. And for all we knew, the vehicle could be bugged, with our enemies listening in to every word since we left the security of our home and lab fortress.

My own mind was distracted as well, still trying to grapple with everything we had recently witnessed and experienced. I had trouble giving Sara the attention she now craved and certainly deserved.

"So we got invited at the last minute? How?"

"I told you. We made good friends with the tour operator today and he has all kinds of connections with bigwigs throughout the city." The traffic was heavy in Manhattan, and vehicles constantly buzzed past us on both sides. Drivers occasionally blasted their horns as other cars burst in line ahead of them.

"And they wanted us to come to a UN function? Us? We're not dignitaries."

"No, but we are friends of a friend of dignitaries."

"And this friend is someone I'll like?"

"Absolutely!" I assured her. "You'll love him. We had quite the adventure together earlier in the day, and he was wining and dining us like royalty on his yacht."

"And he's even fixing Brexxie up with a blind date?"

"Yup."

"Do you know anything about her? Who it is?"

"Not much. She's a board-certified surgeon at the Memorial Sloan-Kettering Cancer Center."

"That's the oldest private cancer center in the world, isn't it?"

Out the window, I saw a middle-aged woman driving a Volvo shoot her middle finger at a yellow cab which pulled out of a side alley right in front of her. Not a good omen for the evening ahead. "Yes, and the largest. She speaks about a dozen languages and specializes in helping patients from abroad coming here specifically for cancer treatment."

Sara looked impressed. "Sounds like a real match! Do you know what she looks like?"

"Bill emailed Brex a picture. She seems cute. Fairly short, but just a little taller than Brex."

He overheard that and looked up from his handheld. "Not tonight! I'm wearing my four-inch heel lifts tonight. And yes, she looks cute. Why do you ask?"

"I'm just a little nervous, Brex. And excited. I'm just curious about everything and worried we might not fit in."

I glanced at our driver. He seemed cool and collected... and most of all quiet. The perfect chauffer. I shrugged. "I agree with you about that, sweetie. We won't fit in and we'll likely never see any of them again except for Bill Higgins and maybe his date and Brexxie's. It's a whole different world."

Brex snorted his agreement. "Yes, dear Jacks, a different world far colder and crueler than ours."

Sara seemed shocked. "Why do you say that, Brexxie?"

He put his phone down completely, screen side down on his lap. "The UN has a lot of solidly democratic, free, first-world countries as members. Many of those governments do fine charitable work worldwide, helping impoverished third-world countries improve their economies, standards of living, and so on. But an awful lot of unsavory tyrannical countries are also members."

"Who thought it was a good idea to invite everyone to the club, so to speak? It sounds as sensible as having the police and the mob all be in the same social club."

I noted the chauffer glanced at us in the rearview mirror when he heard that. I couldn't read anything in his expression. A bit self-consciously, I laughed. "That's a good one, honey. I don't know the whole history, but coming out of World War I, our then-president, Woodrow Wilson, helped promote the League of Nations. That didn't last long, so as World War II was about to break out a couple of decades later, our president then, Franklin Delano Roosevelt, worked with other world leaders to initiate a United Nations."

Our chauffer seemed bored and turned back to the road. We were on the FDR Drive heading north, and I could see at least a mile of auto lights stretching out ahead of us.

She shook her head. "There must have been more than just politicians behind it. I'm guessing some wealthy financiers who would see the economic advantages to having more open global connections."

"I'm not sure about their motivations, but America's wealthiest family, the Rockefellers, bought and then donated the property for the UN headquarters here in Manhattan that we're about to see tonight."

"You'd think people smart enough to reach the top in politics and finance would know enough to have basic decency standards for those invited to join the club."

I could see what I thought was the top of the main UN tower coming into view. "Agreed. I've read things in the press which would curl your hair. UN peace forces sent to primitive nations to keep warring tribes apart, but some of whom spend their off-hours raping local children. Senior UN officials raking in riches for themselves in international oil deals meant to stabilize world economies. Real nice, sweet stuff like that."

Sara gasped. "What an odd mix of good and bad."

Brex lifted his eyebrows. "Kind of like mixing flour and sugar on the one hand with cement, barn scrapings, and dust on the other, all into one giant baked cake. The good ingredients don't make the cake safe and edible because the bad ones keep ruining nearly everything."

"I think you nailed it, Brexxie," I said. It was the UN tower, the Secretariat Building. We were almost there.

Sara looked a bit shocked. "I'm not so sure I want to go tonight, then."

"Don't worry, sweetie. Just realize it's a different world there. But anyone educated and polished enough to make it into a UN delegation, even if from a totalitarian nation where the citizens lack all freedom, has enough sense to act civilized in public. It's just when they are voting for evil, trying to take down the free countries, and oppressing the folks in their own lands back home that their true colors show. They'll smile at you tonight and make small talk and share a cocktail with you, but you'll never see how they act when they go home and rule over their own citizens."

"I'm beginning to wish I had stayed home," Sara moaned.

"Too late. We're here."

Bill Higgins personally met us at the curb and opened the door to let Sara out. I smiled at him and was happy to see Wanda, looking considerably more relaxed and mellow now, still at his side.

And just behind the two of them stood a petite but quite lovely young lady. She had lustrous brown hair cut short— doubtless to make it easier to scrub up for surgery. Her eyes were also brown, large, and with a curious, wide-open expression as if she wanted to know everything about everything and just couldn't wait to find out.

Brex noticed and hopped out of the car as fast as he could, re-holstering his phone on the way.

Smiling, I joined the crowd after giving our driver a tip larger than I could really afford. But what the heck, the ride here, and hopefully the ride home if we lived that long, would be most likely the one big splurge into chaufferdom that we'd ever take.

Bill had already introduced the two blind dates, and as I sauntered over he introduced me, too, to Linda Cesnick. Then, hand in hand, Bill and Wanda led the way towards the party entrance. Brex and Linda chattered amiably as they made their way next, a cautious two feet or so between them as they walked.

Sara and I came last, my arm around her and she sighing as she leaned into my chest. "Ain't love grand, sweetie?" she asked.

"Yes, it is, my darling, yes, it is."

I could overhear part of Brex's conversation with the first date he'd ever had, so far as I knew.

"So, I understand you speak a multiplicity of languages?" he asked.

"*Ja, natürlich!*"

"*Sprechen Sie Urdu?*"

"Of course." She returned to English. "Doesn't everyone?"

Brex was taken aback, and I couldn't help but snigger a little.

Linda played with her hair. "I've been dying to meet you for ages! I attended a urology conference in Kona, Hawaii last year and one paper addressed your research several times!"

"And which research was that, my dear?"

"Your advances in remote tele-microsurgery tools. Astounding! I signed up on the spot for a special training course at Weill Cornell to learn more about it!"

"Oh, that! Just something I got excited about one weekend when reading about the need to bring advanced medical techniques to remote locations around the world. I did what little I could and then moved on to the next topic. You know, I spend most of my time working with my lifelong buddy Jack Rigalto, here. The one you just met, he and his devoted wife behind us now."

"Oh, really? So you're not interested primarily in medicine?"

"My interests are literally infinite, my dear. But right now, we are working on a different kind of project with which we might be able to use your help."

We were leaving the parking area and approaching the well-lit party entrance, with throngs of beautiful ladies in stunning evening gowns and mostly dashing—but sometimes rather old and feeble—gentlemen in tuxedos. A band somewhere inside played evening dinner music, a bit too loud for my taste, and from within I could hear slightly in-toxicated voices talking, also a bit too loudly and with artifi-cial enthusiasm.

"Oh, really? What exactly?"

"There are three particular individuals we hope to meet tonight: one Canadian from Quebec, one Frenchman, and one German. When we converse, it might be helpful if you could note any changes in their speech patterns, use of slang or idiomatic phrases, sidebar comments to colleagues in their own languages, anything which might indicate un-ease with us and our questions."

She looked cross as her cheeks flushed and eyes nar-rowed. "Oh, I get it. You're putting me on with one of Bill Higgins' famous gags. I'm supposed to think I'm in a spy movie or something like that. Well, you've got the wrong girl for that, Doctor Herndon. I don't do James Bond. I spend my life helping cancer victims from abroad get the care they need."

"Wait, Linda, I didn't... I mean..."

But she now stood at least five feet from him as Bill produced our six invites and the bouncer at the entrance waved us all inside.

Linda glanced quickly around the large room—perhaps 100 regally dressed guests, most holding Champagne or martini glasses in their elegant hands, finely attired waiters and waitresses bearing trays of drinks or canapes, and a string quartet on a small stage at the far side of the ball-room. Overhead an enormous glass chandelier filled the room with sparkling light.

She settled on the large glass doors on the right wall, which opened to a terrace overlooking the East River. Even from where I was standing, I could see it looked lovely out there, with a clear, cool sky and a nearly full moon hanging over Roosevelt Island on the other side of the river. She stormed over to one of the doors and slipped outside.

Sara rushed to Brexxie's side. "Stay here, Brex. Let me go talk to her." She darted off as fast as she could with high heels on.

I drew close to Brex. "What happened, buddy?"

He looked perplexed and hurt, his pale lips thinner than usual. "I'm not really sure. I think because we share so many things in common, I assumed we would agree on everything."

"Ah," I said knowingly, thinking back over the thousands of times I had made that same basic mistake, even with the wife I had known for decades. "That's the first rule of male-female relationships, Brexxie. Never assume anything. In-depth communication is the only key to clarity, and even then you'll get it wrong half the time."

He still looked sour. "Not that old canard about the man always being wrong and the woman always being right... even when she's wrong, she's always right."

"No, Brex, I'm not talking about internet jokes and memes. It's just basic reality that no two people, no matter how close, are going to agree on everything or see everything the same way."

Speaking of *seeing*, I suddenly realized that I'd been so focused on Brex that I had lost sight of Sara. Presumably she had followed Linda out to the terrace, but I had neglected to actually watch her do so.

And suddenly we all in the ballroom heard a scream from that area outside the glass doors.

A woman's scream.

17

The View From the Terrace

It didn't sound to me like Sara's voice screaming. She wasn't much of a screamer. If it was just the two of us having an argument, she tended rather to lower her voice and enunciate clearly and perfectly, as if addressing a nincompoop. When she did yell, it was more of a loud shout than an unrestrained scream. In the few times we had faced serious mortal danger together, I had never heard her scream either. I was more likely to hear gunfire or grunts and the force of blows as she personally engaged an enemy with martial arts.

But I wasn't going to wait around inside the ballroom to find out who had screamed. Whoever it was out there might need my help, so I ran straight towards the glass doors, hearing Brexxie's softer footfalls right behind me.

I flung open one of the doors, as did a couple of the security people in the ballroom and a handful of dignitaries, and burst onto the terrace, to see Sara with her arms around Linda, who looked as if in shock. The two of them were looking north, along the Manhattan shore of the East River, the grassy park areas at the top of the UN complex, and Linda had her hands clasped to the sides of her head.

I scanned in the direction they seemed to be looking. Yet another of the sights I was starting to get eerily familiar with—a shimmering window in the dark sky, this time descending all the way to the ground.

I looked closer and could see pouring out of that window, into our world, column after column of what resembled organized troops. They seemed to just materialize out of the thin night air, but hit the ground running in an organized and controlled way, like soldiers pouring out of landing craft at D-Day on the beaches of Normandy.

Yet these guys didn't look altogether like soldiers, for they wore not true uniforms but rather what looked more like vaguely similar garb of their own choosing. It was mostly clothes made of dark cloth, and they wore various kinds of masks to disguise their facial features, often just ordinary-looking black bandanas over their noses and mouths, with dark caps on their heads so that not much more than the eyes showed.

All this took place no more than a hundred or so yards from us, but whatever threat these folks posed, if any, didn't seem directed towards us. They paid us no attention, but rather looked to some leaders on the ground who motioned towards them, barked orders in a tongue I didn't understand, and handed various items to these new arrivals as they passed by on their way into the dark city in huge clusters, each of which followed an apparent sub-leader. Some were given signs, but I couldn't read them from this distance and with so little light and mostly shadows where the writing was. Others were given what looked like simple weapons such as crowbars, hammers, and baseball bats.

All of us stood and stared, silent and motionless for several seconds, maybe a minute or two. I glanced to my left to see Brex at my side. "Must be hundreds of them," I whispered.

"I counted eight hundred and seventy-two, to be exact, since I got here. But I have no idea how many may have passed before I got a good look. Possibly thousands came through before Linda or anyone else on the balcony noticed them."

Both of us headed towards the girls.

As the last of the troops moved out and the window closed into a twinkling final glimpse of light, as if from a distant firefly, Sara turned to us. "Now I know what you and Little Sara were talking about. You all weren't hallucinating."

"No, we weren't," I said. "The difference was in both prior cases, we were forcibly drawn through the window and were caught up into the action on the other side. This is the first time we've seen it the other way around, with figures from the other side emerging into our world."

Linda dropped her hands and turned slowly towards us. She seemed still a little shaken but had largely recovered her composure. She looked straight into Brexxie's eyes as if trying to read him. "So I *am* in a spy movie, then? That certainly wasn't a Bill Higgins prank."

Brex sighed. "No, it certainly wasn't."

"It's real? Not one of David Copperfield's magic tricks, like where he made the Statue of Liberty supposedly disappear?"

"No."

She looked at me next.

I shook my head.

"Then why are all the UN people just standing around, as if this were completely normal? Why aren't they getting all perturbed and calling the police or something?"

I pursed my lips. "That's what we're here to find out. That's why Brex was asking for your help a few minutes ago."

Sara touched her arm like a discreet feather. "Linda, I don't know what's going on either, but it's real. And I can tell you this: if there is one person here who can do anything about it, it is Breslin Herndon, your blind date for this evening. I've known him for nearly twenty-five years, and you can trust him with your life. And I think he can use your help."

Linda looked at Sara questioningly, and Sara nodded.

Linda turned to Brex. "Can we start over again?"

"Of course."

"Okay, I'm game. But only to help people, not hurt them. I'm a healer and I don't believe in violence for any reason."

"Understood. I'm not much into violence myself. I usually leave that up to this big lug here." He pointed at me. "My bodyguard and lifelong best friend."

I corrected him. "Buddy. We're just buddies."

Linda laughed, and we all headed back inside.

I held us guys back a couple of paces. "We're buddies, Brex. Just buddies. Guys don't have best friends. Only girls go all gaga about BFFs."

He looked up at me with question marks in his eyes. "Why shouldn't men have best friends?"

"I didn't say they shouldn't. They just don't. That's just the way it is."

"Maybe that's just you and how you were brought up. Your dad was always off working on the Gulf oil rigs as a blue-collar, greasy-hands-on roustabout, and taught you to be tough as a Louisiana gator."

"No, it's basic evolutionary theory."

His eyes flew wide. "You're talking science to *me*?"

I shrugged. "Think back to the cavemen days or even the cradle of civilization in the Ubaid period that we've experienced firsthand. Females needed tight, very close and hopefully permanent connections with other females to help during birth and raising the young in the tribe's cave or village. Having a 'best' friend could make the difference between surviving and not."

"You're explaining science *to me*? Yeah, I know all about it. While females were tied to the tribal home and each other, the guys were out scavenging on their own for food or occasionally clumping together in groups to hunt down a wooly mammoth or buffalo to feed the whole tribe. They worked as a team, where the one-on-one connections were less important but the ability to work in coordination with all the other guys was paramount."

I nodded. "Especially during the nearly constant tribal warfare of the period. Your connection was to the team, your tribal army, but not to one special man. You had to be able to see the loss of a comrade to your left, but still just step over his dead body and join the comrade next in line. The important thing was that all worked together as a team to protect what they cherished most, the people who depended upon them: their wives and children. All the warriors were buddies, but no particular one could be special because you had to face his possible loss at tomorrow's hunt or battle and still be able to function."

"You're still special to me, dear Jacks. We don't live in a primitive, barbaric time now."

I threw up my hands. "Maybe, Brexxie, maybe it appears that way right now. But it seems to me that barbarianism is right around the corner, that Troy has opened up its city gates to that cool-looking horse, and that brutes are surging among us even now!"

He looked somber and serious. "Don't worry, Jacks. If worse comes to worst, and you don't make it through this crisis, I'll be able to step over your dead body and continue taking care of Sara and Sara."

For a moment I stood speechless, staring at him, trying to come up with the right words. "I know, buddy. I can count on you."

He looked up at me with an endearing expression. Then he lightly punched my shoulder with his small fist. "That's how you do it, right? Not with words."

I lightly tapped him back, but pulled my punch dramatically, so as not to hurt him. "That's how you do it. We're warriors."

Before we could even reach the glass doors, a beep-beep sound came from his smartphone and Brex pulled it out for a look.

He seemed speechless, so I asked, "What is it?"

"A huge mob of 'youths' has just taken over Wall Street. Breaking windows, setting cars on fire, assaulting any unlucky bystander caught in their path. The NYPD is vastly outnumbered and has lost control."

By this time, everyone had gone back inside except for our party of four.

And one gentleman just barely in front of us. When he reached the door, instead of opening it he blocked it. He turned to face the four of us.

I recognized him immediately—Jacque Bouchard of the Canadian delegation, last seen by us via Brexxie's spy satellite, giving instructions to The Iceman and the other two goons who assaulted all of us back at our secure house and lab.

"What did you do to The Iceman? Our specialists say it is impossible to turn a living human into a mineralized statue."

Brex snapped like a rubber band. "Most experts would say it is impossible to import thousands of barbarians from a more primitive time into the modern world... but, there you go."

"Ha! Thousands? No, millions. Thousands of millions. A billion just for starters."

The numbers were becoming too large to seem real any longer. I knew the current American population was something on the order of one-third of a billion. If a billion more joined us, that would quadruple our population. Everything would be four times as crowded. Everything. And all resources such as housing, food, clean water, and air would become completely strained beyond the capacity for comprehensive re-supply.

It was a recipe for chaos. And obviously by design. Deliberate invasion.

"What do you want, Bouchard?" Brex snapped.

"Well, what I really want is to watch your faces fall into despair as you see your civilization crumble around you. I want to watch your agony as you see everything you care about torn from you and you must kneel before me, crawl, and beg for the crumbs which even allow you to live."

"*Monstre!*" spat Linda.

"*Parlez-vous Francais?*"

"*Oui.*"

"*Vous parlez français avec un accent américain.*"

"What's he going on about?" I whispered to Brex. "What's he saying?"

"Nothing. He's just being a creep."

Sara pushed closer, her fists clenched. "How dare you threaten us as Americans here on our own soil!"

Bouchard laughed at that. "This is UN property and legally considered non-American soil. It is you who are out of place here. You have left America and are a foreigner here. In fact, your presence here is no longer desirable in any way. I hereby negate your invitations, given out under false pretenses in the first place, and you have exactly three minutes to vacate the premises before I call the police to report *you* for breaking the law and failing to respect UN territorial boundaries!"

I eased in front of Sara. "I don't yet fully understand what you are up to, but our government is going to nail you for this."

He laughed heartily. "I and my colleagues have broken no law. We are implementing the UN resettlement program and bringing refugees into this country. All quite legal. There's nothing you can do about that."

"So you think it's legal to send a hit squad to our house to kill us?"

"*Kill* you? My, but you are stupider than I thought. They were messengers sent to warn you."

"Warn us about what? What was the message?" I asked.

"Forget it. It's too late. You killed the very messengers sent to protect you. How do you Anglos put it? Ah, yes. 'Don't shoot the messenger'."

I looked at Brex. "We shot the messenger?"

He muttered glumly, "We shot the messenger."

18

The Iceman's Message

At a single snap of Bouchard's fingers, several bouncers appeared and escorted us from the ballroom out to the parking lot.

Meanwhile, as we hesitantly walked through the alien space, I wasn't sure where Bill Higgins and Wanda were, nor whether they were getting ejected also, but I wasn't going to try to find out now. I did grab a couple of canapes, though, as we passed a tray on a serving table. Ones chosen at random wouldn't be spiked.

Many dignitaries glared at us as we trudged away. I caught the eye of one older matron in a flowing gown and she quickly turned to her martini, taking a slow sip and then looking at her partner, whose eyelids drooped as if he'd had one too many martinis already.

As we headed back towards the parking lot, Linda muttered, "Well, that was embarrassing. Brex, you sure know how to show a girl a good time."

I laughed, but then I caught a glimpse of his face and realized he hadn't taken it as a joke. The music and forced laughter behind us grew softer with distance, and traffic sounds increased as we approached the auto area.

Sara loudly cleared her throat. "I've got a great idea: why don't we all go for coffee somewhere and you guys tell us who this Iceman character was and your best guess as to what his special message was."

"How about Starbucks?" I suggested.

Linda screwed up her face. "They make some luscious lattes and frappes and such, but I can't take all that sugar. Want to go to my place? It's only a few blocks south of here."

The artificial lights seemed garish out here after the soft glow in the ballroom. I snickered.

"What's so funny?" she demanded.

"Not really funny as in ha ha. Just ironic."

"What is?"

"You don't care much for sugar, which is fine by me. I drink my coffee plain black myself. But for some of us, too much sugar is never enough." We were close enough to the parking area where I could smell spilt motor oil and exhaust fumes.

Linda took hold of Sara's arm. "Don't tell me you're one of those chocoholic types always scarfing down cookies and candy and pie?"

Sara gulped. "No, not me…"

Linda realized her faux pas. "Oops! Sorry!"

And I realized mine as well.

I found the raw honk of auto horns distracting as Linda led us to her car, a silver Lexus GX460. She had the driving dexterity and elan of an Indy 500 professional as she expertly zipped through the handful of blocks to her home.

She had a nice place in a beautiful condominium building on 63rd Street, directly above the waterfront. From the windows of her spacious living room, I could see the FDR Drive below, then the dark East River, and on the far side Roosevelt Island.

Within minutes, she brought out coffee and a tray filled with a variety of creamers and sweeteners. All of us tried not to look as Brexxie applied several of each until his cup looked as if filled with some kind of milkshake.

Linda settled back with her cup. "I realize that if we are in James Bond land that there are some things you guys can't divulge, but I am all ears if there is something you can talk about. What I saw happen on the UN grounds tonight certainly wasn't a secret."

Sara added, "I'm especially curious about The Iceman's intended message, assuming Bouchard was telling the truth."

Brex and I looked at each other. Nothing we knew at this point was actually classified.

I sipped and cradled my cup. "Well, Bouchard seemed quite open about what they are up to, and you saw it yourself, at least one small part of it. The secret part is *why* they are so intent on flooding American territory with as many folks as they can cram in, just as fast as possible, including untold numbers of barbarians from the distant past."

"I'll bite," said Linda. "Why?"

Sara placed her cup down. "Usually the best way to understand a seemingly inexplicable action is to follow the money trail. Who's making a profit off it?"

I nodded.

Brex took a long sip of his foamy latte. "Good coffee, Linda."

"Thanks." She didn't elaborate, just sat looking at him patiently but expectantly.

Brex leaned back, stretched his arms and hands, and cracked his knuckles. "I can't answer that question without some background first to provide context." He turned to Sara. "Same for explaining The Iceman. You first have to know where he came from."

"We're all ears, Brex," I said. "No one can tell it like you can."

He took another long sip until all attention focused entirely on him. "Have you ever heard of the famous John B. Calhoun study published in *Scientific American* in 1962?"

The two women both shook their heads.

"It was called 'Population Density and Social Pathology'."

"Tell us about it."

"Well, even to get into that, I must back up a little. You'll recall that for about the first one hundred to one hundred and fifty years of our nation's history, we were just one among many nations around the world emerging slowly from a largely agrarian society into a fully industrialized one. Then after World War I we had the so-called Roaring Twenties, when it seemed prosperity was now available for all and would probably be permanent."

Linda rolled her eyes. "Well, I know that sentiment didn't last long, because we had the stock market crash of 1929, followed by the Great Depression. My grandfather was one of those who lost everything pretty much overnight and literally jumped out of his office window on Wall Street."

Brex nodded. "In those days, America was just one among many nations, more or less equal in terms of international power. Except for Great Britain, of course. 'Brittania rules the waves', as one of their patriotic, martial songs gladly proclaims. And the famous saying of Lord Salisbury, 'The sun never sets on the British Empire', was literally true, with their colonies and territories spread all over the world."

"Anyway..." I broke in, trying to speed this up.

"Anyway, then came World War II and we emerged as the richest, most powerful nation on earth, the only major one which had suffered no direct damage of any lasting consequence on the homeland itself during the war, but had rather built up an astonishing number of new factories able to create a total output more prodigious than anything ever seen before on earth. We were number one and everyone knew it."

"And..." I nudged him again.

"The so-called Greatest Generation had suffered through the Depression, won the dreadful world war, and built the richest nation the world had ever seen. But everyone began to worry what would happen to the national character when the baby boomers, the ones born after the war, grew up with an unearned affluence and bounty they never had to work to secure. I don't mean their individual and family welfare, of course. Folks still had to go to school, learn skills, and earn their way with jobs. I'm talking about the fate of the nation as a whole."

"I'm sorry, Brex, but you're taking too long. Don't be such a professor. This isn't one of your MIT classes." I turned to the ladies, "The bottom line was people began to worry that if hard times had produced strong people who fought through the worst to build good times, would those good times produce a catastrophe of weak character in the next generation or two which would wipe out all the gains."

"Oh," said Linda, "you're talking about the cyclical view of history, the rise and fall of cultures and nations and empires."

"Correctamundo," said Brex. Then he glared at me. "You said I could tell it best, me jocko. Don't say that and

then interrupt me every ten seconds and try to tell it better."

I looked down. "Sorry, Brex. You're Dr. Brains. Go
ahead."

"Correctamundo. I'm Dr. Brains and you are Mr.
Brawn. I don't tell you how to fight."

"Yes, you do!"

Linda chuckled. "Dr. Brains and Mr. Brawn. I can see
that! And I like it. It fits."

Brex smiled. "Anyway. So Calhoun created a society in
his lab where the subjects didn't have to work at all. It was
a prosperous colony where all needs were filled all the time
and there was plenty of everything. No deprivation or want."

"Wait," interrupted Sara. "You mean he raised human
kids like that?"

"Oh, no, sorry. That's not what I meant. In Calhoun's
view, America's post-war prosperity had already produced
that situation for the entire new generation. Calhoun created a parallel situation with mice growing up in a place of
unlimited prosperity where he could completely control the
set-up. At first the mice seemed happy. They ate and drank
and had sex and multiplied and generally acted as if nothing they did had consequences because plenty was the
name of the game and it would just always magically be
that way."

Linda muttered, "I'm beginning to sense what went
wrong with that."

"Oh, yes, everything went wrong. I mean everything! Ul-
timately the mouse colony completely destroyed itself, but
at first it just looked like manageable problems such as
overpopulation and crowding, the formation of gangs among
aimless young males, the breakdown of normal courtship
rituals and mouse family organization. But then all restraints fell off and there was violence and forced sex and
abandonment of one's own young, with mortality rates of
up to ninety-six percent, and eventually they all just died
off."

"How horrible!" exclaimed Sara.

"Yes, indeed. It was," I said. "And I think the general
parallels with the rise and fall of human societies are obvious. Thank you for telling us the story, Brexxie. No one
could tell it better than you."

He beamed. "Thank you, my dear Jacks."

But Linda pursed her lips. "I certainly see the parallels between Calhoun's study with mice and all the decline in Western civilization in recent decades, but how does all that tie in with The Iceman, his message, and what the UN is doing now?"

"Everything, absolutely everything! We never did know for sure for whom Iceman was working. Maybe just for himself. Maybe he was freelance and worked for whomever paid the most. Maybe for some shadowy globalist group."

Sara grunted. "Follow the money. Whoever was raking it in based on The Iceman's actions is the one likeliest to have been giving him orders and paying him."

Brex pondered her words. "Sara, that's a good point, but it doesn't narrow it down sufficiently to be certain exactly who. A lot of globalist types make money when chaos increases around the world."

"Like whom?"

"Arms dealers. Investors in supplies of oil and other energy forms, precious metals, essential raw materials to keep civilization afloat. Anything people need and suddenly get desperate over when they realize the supply is dwindling."

"Back to The Iceman," I encouraged.

"We may never determine who was paying him at this point. But he had his own motivations beyond high pay for secret work. He was intimately familiar with the Calhoun study and saw in it a blueprint for what he wanted to do with America."

"Wait a sec," broke in Sara. "He didn't see that as a cautionary tale to avoid?"

"No, he saw it as the very thing he wanted to implement so that he could destroy America."

"He *wanted* to destroy America by throwing it into utter chaos?"

"Yes."

"Why?"

"As the famous saying goes, 'Some people just want to watch the world burn'."

I drained the rest of my coffee. "Some people believe the only way to avoid future conflicts among nations, such as that seen in the world wars of the last century, is to get rid of nations themselves. Throw open all the borders and have just one global government for everyone. And the only way to accomplish that is to destroy the one nation powerful enough to stand in their way, namely America."

I noted that Brex had finished his milk shake of a coffee and was furtively sneaking Peanut M&Ms out of the bags in his pockets, quietly slipping them one at a time into his mouth.

Linda had her eyes on me and didn't seem to notice.

I continued, "And the easiest way to destroy America is from within, by applying the Calhoun study as a battle plan, so to speak, since no other power from outside America has yet emerged that seemed strong enough to destroy her from outside."

Sara's eyes flashed with anger. "That strikes me as downright evil, malicious, and reprehensible."

I glanced at Sara. "I certainly agree with that, but to be fair, the other side would apply those adjectives to us, believing we are standing in their way of creating permanent global peace."

Linda's expression turned very sour. "Maybe they believe that, or at least claim to believe it, but it's the biggest pile of nonsensical bull crap I've ever heard. Whether the world has a couple of hundred separate nations or one single supranational government won't change what the French author Émile Zola called 'La Bête humaine' or 'the human beast', the innate corruption in people, what religious folks call 'original sin'."

"Exactly," said Brex. "There would be more chaos, not less. More tyranny, not less. Incalculable human suffering as the new globalist leaders would prove Lord Acton's dictum that 'Power corrupts, and absolute power corrupts absolutely'."

Linda lowered her voice almost to a whisper. "The ultimate plot for world conquest, but where the ancient Greeks and Romans failed, where the more modern Nazis and communists failed, these current globalists seem to have a real chance at pulling it off. The headlines in any newspaper any day herald how much progress they've made."

Sara opened her mouth, closed it, then tried again. "Watching the world burn... someone or some group will gain incalculable wealth and power by lighting the match and adding fuel to that fire."

I nodded.

Sara raised her eyebrows and looked straight at Brex. "I'm following all this, but still have no clue what Iceman's message for you guys was."

Brex glanced at me and shrugged. "We'll never know for sure, since he is dead and his apparent boss or colleague Bouchard refuses to say, but my guess is they wanted to enlist us on their side. I had just observed, through a Schimmerplotz encounter, their plan to import untold numbers of Ubaidian barbarians into our current space-time, and had just reported it to our superiors, when they showed up. They probably wanted us on their side instead of against it."

I nodded at Brex. "But when we obviously refused to play ball, they realized our sympathies lay with America and against their plan."

Linda let out a deep breath. "Bouchard can't be the mastermind behind all this. He's just a well-placed flunkie who's doing the bidding of someone else way above his pay grade."

I noted out of the corner of my eye that Brexxie had reached into his pocket yet one more time, but came up empty.

"Excuse me, Linda," he said. "You wouldn't happen to have any Peanut M&Ms, would you?

19

Utopia At Last

At Linda's place we were having a good time, but Sara kept dropping big hints about how we needed to get back home and relieve the babysitter, her sister Tara. Both Sara and I kept trying to catch Brex's eye to see if he wanted to return with us or stay behind for some alone time with Linda.

We couldn't grab his attention because he had all eyes fixed on his date for the evening. When she got up to clean away all the dirty dishes, he followed close behind like a new puppy. He watched her every move and made eye contact whenever possible. He seemed fascinated by every golden syllable which tumbled from those ruby lips.

I was thinking they should just get a room, but then I realized she had several rooms right there. We were the left thumbs standing in the way of young love and needed to get moving. Finally I blurted out, "Listen, Brex, we've got to get back home, but do you want to go with us now or stay a little longer here?"

We looked at Linda, and her expression seemed ambivalent. I hated to put her on the spot, but we needed to have some kind of decision.

She reached out and took Brex's hand, and I swear I saw him shiver. She said, "It's not too late for us swinging singles. Let the old married fuddy-duddies go home if they need to. You can stay another hour or two if you want. I have some thirties and forties jazz records in the original vinyl, 78 RPM releases, in case you're interested."

"Gosh, Linda, that sounds great. But would you mind if we do that another time? I'm really tired just now, but I'd love to see you again another day."

She shrugged and looked a bit disappointed, I thought, as the three of us started moving towards the door. "Suit yourself. You have my number."

At the door, Sara and I hurried out but then lingered in the corridor to give them a private goodbye moment.

Brex paused in the doorway and looked nervously at us, then turned back to her. "Linda, would you mind if—?"

Alarmed, Sara poked him in the ribs, and when he looked at her, she silently mouthed the words "Don't ask, just do it. She wants to kiss you. Trust me," where Linda couldn't see.

He closed his eyes too soon as he started to lean toward her, and his mouth caught only the top edge of her head. A faceful of brown hair. Instead Linda cradled his face with both hands, leaned forward, and gave him a brief kiss on the cheek.

He stammered, "Guh, goodnight, sweetie," then turned and joined us.

Once the elevator doors had safely closed behind us, I patted his shoulder. "Way to go, dude!"

He beamed and looked to me three inches taller. "You can be my best man, my dear Jacks. Yes, yessiree, you can."

We asked the doorman to hail us a cab and waited on the bricks of the driveway as a chill wind blew in from the East River.

Then I saw it. Another floating, shimmering window, this time moving straight for us. Well, straight for me, anyway. I didn't see any point in trying to run; I had a premonition that I was destined for this. But I shoved Sara out of the window's way as it was about to envelope us, barking for her to get home as soon as possible.

I grabbed Brex and held onto his upper arm. "Sorry, Brex, I don't think I can survive this without you. You've gotta come with me."

He had just enough time to shout to Sara, "See if Linda will go back with you to the safe house. She may be in danger!"

I saw Sara nod, and then we sailed instantaneously through a vast void and found ourselves in a strange yet also vaguely familiar environment as we landed on the edge of some kind of cesspool.

At least it smelled like a cesspool. There was a body of water on our left, a dilapidated cluster of piers and old boats, and a massive electrified fence on our right. It was dark, with nothing but moonlight for illumination, but I could see vaguely and certainly hear a bustling, groaning throng on the other side of that fence.

I couldn't help but think it looked, sounded, and smelled like Yankee Stadium might if an enormous crowd had assembled for a game but then been trapped inside for days, unable to find relief or escape. Come to think of it, I remembered pics of the New Orleans Superdome after Hurricane Katrina in 2005 which reminded me of this.

I turned to Brex. "Where the heck are we?"

"You don't want to know."

"Well, yeah, I kinda do."

"Jacks, how many times have I told you to pay attention to all the details of your environment?"

I turned slowly, making a 360 degree turn. The body of water which I'd first noted looked like a river, but one filled, absolutely filled, with reeking, rotting bodies, both human and animal. I was glad for just dim light, for I didn't really want to see those bloated carcasses clearly. *What horrible disaster has struck this place?* "Brex, it looks like the aftermath of a tsunami, like pics I've seen from Japan or Malaysia in the news."

"Look closer, my friend. Anything familiar about this river, these boats?"

Then I noted the moonlight flickering off the glass top of a yacht tied to the nearby pier, bobbing gently in the waves. "The *Manhattan II*? We're on Pier 62 again on the Hudson?"

"I knew you could do it. Note the clues, then put them together into a pattern that makes sense."

"We're still in Manhattan, not back in Mesopotamia?"

"Remember my theory about Schimmerplotzes being brief collisions among adjacent dimensions moving through time and space? It's mostly random and unpredictable where you might go."

"Of course. So we're in Manhattan... but when?"

"That is, of course, the right question. Clearly nothing so remotely disastrous as this has happened in the past we knew, so we are in—"

"The future?"

"Maybe our future... or maybe just an alternative dimension with its own future distinct from our own."

"Well, there are no lights visible on the yacht, but do you think someone could be home?"

"Let's find out."

As we conversed and made noise and moved around, the crowd on the other side of the fence emitted more grunts and cries. Clusters began to form at the fence, and one emaciated, human-like thing about 20 feet from us reached out and took hold of the double chain link. Immediately, bright arcs of electricity passed from the metal throughout his body, flinging him back among his fellows with a horrible stench of burnt flesh stinging my nostrils.

With hideous shrieks of feral joy, some of the pitiable creatures around him began to literally tear him apart and munch on his fried remains.

"Cannibals, Brex? Are they zombies?"

"I think not. The whole concept of zombies is pretty stupid when you think about it. How can someone be undead from a futuristic virus or whatever? You get a virus and either recover or die from it. The word 'undead' is a ridiculous misnomer in the first place. Someone is either alive or is dead. There's no third alternative... at least not in our universe."

"So why are zombie movies and TV shows so wildly popular?"

"Because they tap into one of our most primitive fears and archetypes, namely, the dread of being at the mercy of an utterly savage and primitive mob of unrestrained, devilish monsters. The feeling of being a weak lamb beset upon by wild, hungry jackals who care not the slightest about your feelings but obey only the lust of their own hunger."

"So, if these are mortals, what has happened to them?"

Some had fed. The unhappy remainder beside the fence

glared at us with hungry and hollow eyes. I stepped further away from the fence, toward the reeking water.

"It reminds me of what happened when communist Stalin deliberately starved the Ukranian populace into submission back in the 1930s. The so-called Holodomor. People resorted to cannibalism to survive. You can see the same throughout history in reports of cities under prolonged siege when their supplies ran out; people lost or abandoned in the wild, like the Donner Party in 1840s America; underfed victims in slave labor camps, and so on."

"So we are not witnessing the aftermath of a natural disaster?" The river smelled even worse than the fence, but it appeared nothing in the water was as interested in consuming us as the emaciated things on the other side of that chain link.

"Not everything is clear to me yet, dear Jacks, but I fear not. I think this is a man-caused disaster. If we can find someone alive in the yacht, we may be able to find out."

"Well, someone has gone to a lot of trouble to protect this pier from the insane mob outside the fence." We walked down the pier to the gangway and I yelled out, "Ahoy, there! Anybody home? May we come aboard?"

I was stunned to see Bill Higgins come cautiously out of the door towards us. At least it reminded me of our friend Bill, but it might be his father or another relative, for he looked at least 20 years older than the man who had taken us to the UN party just a few hours ago in our time.

He held a crowbar in his hands and looked suspicious and fearful at first. Then recognition dawned in his eyes. "Brexxie? Jack Rigalto? I haven't seen you in, what, seven or eight years at least? I thought General Bnindagun had murdered you by now!"

"Bnindagun is still around?" I asked.

"Around? Yeah, he pretty much controls the whole global army now. He's the only seven-star general in the history of the universe, or so he likes to proclaim. He's the commander-in-chief of the Global Unity Army."

"May we come aboard?"

"I guess. We may as well get you out of sight as soon as we can. They'll kill me if they think I'm supporting Waywards."

"Waywards?" Brex asked.

"Yeah, anyone guilty of thinking thoughts against the Global Universalist Party. Not allowed."

We started up the gangway. The stench from the water was stronger this close. I had to ask. "How come you seem to be okay while there is a ravenous mob of cannibals just outside your fence?"

"Oh, yeah. Don't go out there or they'll tear you limb from limb, lick up every corpuscle of blood, and gnaw on every one of your bones. They're the Waywards, the ones the GUP doesn't give a hoot about."

"So how come you seem to be all right, given that you're living in a nightmare of a world?" The yacht rocked slightly as we clambered aboard.

"General Bnindagun said he has fond memories of me not giving him problems like you two did in our previous encounters. He let me live."

"And you're still on the same yacht!"

"Yeah, when he took over, I still had plenty of high-level connections, and they kept me around for whenever one of the new ruling elite wanted a yacht tour of any kind. You see, these days, the GUP leaders at the top control the whole world. Anyone with special skills, abilities, or other resources—anyone who can be of use—is protected and allowed to serve them. The rest of the population, they don't care about and give them nothing. Not even energy use is allowed these days."

We followed Bill into the interior. The light was dim, but I could see the yacht was still well furnished. In fact, some of the fixtures which I recalled as being brass now appeared to be gold. "Not any energy of any kind?"

"Well, nothing beyond what you can supply with your own body. The Party leadership get whatever they want, of course, night and day. They still live in mansions and feast and party all the time. There's a cluster of them living in a special green zone, a secure area in New York. They have other secure clusters in other large coastal cities and capital cities abroad."

I grimaced. "That figures." I looked at the gold and wanted to spit on it. It seemed uglier than brass to me now.

"Servants like me in the second tier get the crumbs left over, and are at least protected from the mobs of dying Waywards. Whenever I host a VIP group on the yacht, one of them just flashes his number on the control screen, and I have full power and everything as long as they want it. But when I'm alone I'm allowed only fifteen minutes a day of electricity so I can prepare meals."

"So everybody else gets bupkis?" asked Brex.

"Sadly, yes. The majority of the populace gets nothing at all, which is why they are rapidly declining as they die off. There are no more cars, trains, subways, airplanes, electricity, light, heating, cooling, appliances, or anything for the masses. We can't afford for them to use that much carbon, so they have to do without."

I felt anger rising within me like lava in a volcano. "Wait a second. In a city like New York, with all the skyscrapers and very hot summers, there is no electricity or air conditioning?"

"Correct. That's why everyone in the third tier abandoned their homes and the survivors who could make it to Central Park or one of the other parks settled there. That mob outside lives in Riverside Park, if you can call that living."

"No, not living at all. Yet not all dead yet, either, at least those out there."

"Well, the bright side of all this, at least according to GUP propaganda, is that the sacrifice of the masses has saved the planet and is restoring all as the new Garden of Eden."

Brex glanced at me and I saw rage in his eyes. "That's how all totalitarian leaders justify everything they do. As Stalin put it, you have to break a few eggs to make an omelette."

I was still shocked by all I was hearing. "How the heck did all this come to happen? Did no one fight back?"

"Sure, a few tried, but they were quickly wiped out. The first order of the GUP elite, when they took over was—"

"Let me guess: gun control."

"Yeah, that was it."

"So now that there's no energy use throughout most of the world, I suppose the climate is golden. No more climate change, right?"

Bill laughed. "Man, that's funny. I missed you guys, you know. It's good to see you again."

"Same here," I said.

Brex nodded. "It's great catching up with you, but the sooner we leave the safer you'll be. We need to get going on the mission we were sent here for."

I could hear some kind of siren in the distance. Headed this way? I couldn't tell yet. I cleared my throat. "Which is?"

"We're going to kill General Bnindagun once and for all."

"That's right," said Bill. "When Jacks killed the primitive one in a different time and place, you said you'd have to deal with him again in the future. I never understood it, but I remember you saying that."

"Can you tell us where he is now and how to get there?"

I nodded grimly, "That's the best idea you've had all day, Brexxie."

"*Sic semper tyrannis.*"

"I know that one," said Bill. "That was a Latin phrase commonly used during the American Revolution. 'Thus always to tyrants', usually implying death. But listen, guys, it's not just the general. He runs the military, but the global dictator over the whole planet is his boss."

"And who might that be?" I asked.

"I don't know. The elite must know, but it's never been revealed to the rest of us. But from what we hear, he is the first trillionaire in the history of the world."

I looked at Brex. "Follow the money, Sara said."

"Looks like she was right."

20

The Dominoes Begin to Fall

It seemed oddly familiar to be rowing a boat on a river again, but this time a modern lifeboat stolen from one of the yachts docked at Pier 62, and this time in the Hudson River filled with more bodies than the Euphrates the day we sailed there.

Brex steered as I put my back into it and rowed, rowed as if I wanted to win an Olympic gold medal. Despite the cool weather along the river in the middle of the night, beads of sweat had broken out on my forehead and my armpits felt moist. I could feel my muscles bulging with each contraction as I rowed and rowed and rowed.

It must have been at least one mile by now, but we had another to go. At least my nostrils had become numb to the smell on the water and I could breathe without wanting to gag.

Bill had told us the New Eden for the GUP elite had been built on the only part of Manhattan Island left largely undeveloped in our day, the woodsy north end beyond Harlem, the area where the Hudson flowed south along the west of the island, and the Harlem River flowed down its east side.

I paused for a moment to catch my breath. "Brex, buddy, General Bnindagun must have all sorts of security and armed personnel guarding him. There's probably a lot of stuff that didn't even exist in our day and that you don't know about. What have we got?"

The lonely splash of my oars was the only sound besides that of my friend's voice. There were almost no lights visible at any point on land. A city that once reveled in light 24 hours a day was now nearly completely dark. I couldn't help but shiver.

"Don't worry, my friend. The general never had someone like me working for him, so there is likely no new development in the seven or eight years after our time that I didn't already anticipate. And you, dear Jacks, have the one person on your side that he doesn't."

"You."

"Yes, me."

"So what do you 'got'? Any more special weapons and devices hidden in that flesh-colored waist pack you carry around under your clothes? That sure helped us in Mesopotamia the other day. And also when that gang of toughs assaulted us."

"But of course."

"And they are?"

"I could spend all night here explaining them to you... but then the general would wake up and be gone on his trip to the GUP World Headquarters in Geneva, as Bill Higgins warned us."

I resigned myself. "Or I could shut my big yap and let you give me what I need when the tactical situation requires it."

"Or you could shut your yap and get on with the mission. One which you are uniquely qualified for and obviously have been summoned for, although by whom is not entirely clear to me yet."

Was Brex playing me or being sincere? "So you think I have unique qualifications?" I could hear a helicopter in the distance and see its light in the sky far away. Possibly a routine patrol or maybe someone starting to look for us. I had no way to know yet, but all my senses were set for full tactical awareness.

"But of course you do, dear Jacks. Everyone knows that. You and I complement each other perfectly. Together we make one superhuman. With my brain and your warrior brawn, not to mention fighting skills and instincts, we are unbeatable."

"Let's hope so."

I started rowing again and soon the enormous fence around New Eden appeared. Clearly it was electrified and could keep out giants, dinosaurs, or starving mobs of desperate Waywards. Luckily there was one break in the otherwise impenetrable fence—the dock area where Bill Higgins would pause long enough for the general and his VIP throng of trusted lieutenants and sexy ladies to embark the *Manhattan II* on their occasional pleasure outing.

I couldn't see it myself, as my back was to it. But Brex was obviously steering the lifeboat in that direction.

"Slow down, my friend. We are almost there and we have to disable the alarm Bill spoke of."

I stopped rowing and let the boat slow to a gradual stop. I strained with all my senses for any hint of danger.

The river rustled behind me, as if Brex dipped a hand into the water, testing it. "Don't forget, the general and his security team probably have no idea that anyone might approach other than a half-dead, zombie-like, starving Wayward. They won't be expecting serious resistance. Anyone capable of that in their space-timeline was slaughtered long ago."

"He thinks he's safe because he's killed off all the real Americans. We are about to show him that it takes only two seriously ticked-off freedom fighters to bring the fire to him!"

"Amen, bro!"

We kept low in the boat, hoping the guards on the inside of the gate wouldn't notice something small on the outside floating idly toward them. Likely they were used to dead bodies and the occasional abandoned watercraft drifting aimlessly around and wouldn't get alarmed unless they saw or heard something atypical.

Lying prone on the boat, I canoe-paddled very slowly the final 30 or so yards to the outside end of the private pier. Brex steered and then tied the boat to the pier while I kept watch on the two armed guards on the inside of the dock area.

As I'd hoped, they didn't pay the little boat any attention. I noted they were smoking and joking and did not have weapons at the ready. Both of them had rifles slung over their shoulders, and at least one sidearm holstered and a knife in a sheath. I couldn't see clearly enough to assess the exact type of weapons, but clearly their tactical awareness was low and military discipline seemed nearly nonexistent.

As we crept silently up the ladder to the pier's surface, I could see more clearly the electrified fence that ran along the edge of the water and extended across the pier, a lone gate atop the planks.

I whispered to Brex, "What do you have to defeat that locked gate?"

"Nothing."

"So how do you propose to get in?"

"You already have everything you need to take out the lock and alarm and the two guards."

"What do you mean?"

"You still have your 1911 Colt .45, right? The one you had in concealed carry when we visited the UN and went to Linda's."

"Well, obviously, and I have my nine-inch Smith and Wesson Special Ops lockback folding knife, too, and a fixed-blade knife strapped to my calf. But what about stealth? I can't just go charging in there like a cowboy, can I?"

"Why not? What's the one thing they likely expect the least?"

"Someone charging directly in like an armed, seriously ticked-off cowboy."

"So that's what we're going to give them. The element of surprise, my dear Jacks. Seize the initiative. Strike the enemy where and when and how he least expects it. That will strike fear in his heart and sow confusion."

"Thanks for the theoretical lesson on Sun Tzu's *The Art of War*. But you're forgetting one key practical concern."

"What's that?"

"If we got in there undetected and started eliminating our foes before anyone was the wiser, we'd improve the numerical odds in our favor."

"Balderdash. If we sow confusion and everyone starts going crazy and firing all at once, they're more likely to shoot each other than us. Friendly fire, remember? Besides, forcing them to show all their cards at once gives me the chance to analyze their capabilities so we know how to hit them where it really hurts."

"Brexxie, sometimes when you say something that at first sounds like something really stupid, it turns out to be really smart."

"One of my talents, dear Jacks. Just one among many."

"And modesty is also one. Don't forget that one."

"How could I? It's one of my best and most apparent!"

Bent over, we eased quickly but quietly toward the electrified gate. While we were still far enough away for the guards not to hear it, I slipped out my .45 and cocked back the slide. At the gate, I aimed through the chain link at the guard with a cigarette in his mouth who was looking vaguely towards the water, pulled the trigger, and he collapsed with the top of his head missing, but the ciggy still in place.

The second guard had been facing away, toward his friend, when the gun blast rang out and his colleague fell to the green lawn. Now he frantically reached to grab the rifle sling off his shoulder and face us. Before he was ready, I sent him to oblivion with another 230-grain bullet.

Like shooting fish in a barrel.

Brex chuckled "Nice shots. That's a seven-round mag, right?"

"Yes. But I have two more."

"Then I'd better get my weapon ready." He pulled up his shirt, found the zipper in his waist pack, and quickly pulled out something. I couldn't see what it was.

Then with a third bullet, I knocked out the lock at the gate and it swung loose. In case the fence remained electrified, I pushed the gate open with an oar from the lifeboat.

We slipped inside.

Then chaos broke loose.

21

Pandemonium

Searchlights burst on atop the New Eden palatial mansion's roof as alarms blared from all four corners of the grounds.

I could hear orders being yelled by unseen humans' voices, and then lines of troops, at least four squads of ten soldiers each, poured out of different doors and began to roam different sectors of the well-kept grounds, with stone pathways, marble fountains, manicured shrubs, and what looked like a two-level swimming pool in the distance, one level raised above the patio deck, with thick glass siding holding the water in, then a raised tubular slide connecting to the lower-level pool, inset below the surface of the patio itself.

More ominously, a row of sharp spikes shot from below ground up about ten feet to form the rails of a new fence surrounding the dock area within the electrified fence, completely hemming us in along the waterfront.

My eyes on the advancing troops, their rifles at the ready, I whispered to Brex, "*This* is what you were hoping for?"

"Exactly! Now they've shown their entire poker hand all at once. Queen high with a couple of deuces and treys."

"And what do we have besides two trapped jokers?"

"We, my dear friend, have one Jack, one king, and three aces."

"Well, he just called, and it's our time to raise or fold."

"Never! Time to secure our hand for the moment and finish the play later."

The item he had retrieved from his pack was still in his hand. I got a closer look as he fiddled with it. It resembled more some kind of mini-bomb or grenade than a futuristic pistol of some sort. About the size of a golf ball, but shiny and metallic.

He tossed it towards the bars of the spiky fence which had just appeared out of nowhere. It hit one of the uprights with a ping and clung there, maybe four or five feet above the ground.

Magnetic.

He tapped my shoulder and turned, running towards the far end of the pier. "Jacks, my friend, we have about ninety seconds to get the boat at least a hundred yards from here. Do you think you can do that for me, buddy?"

I was following him before he spoke. "With one oar tied behind my back," I whispered hoarsely while running to the boat like a quarterback with the ball racing for the goal line. I had the boat untied, and was in position at the oars, when Brex caught up, clambered down the ladder's five steps, and hopped aboard. He steered as I rowed with the power of ten racehorses.

About 30 seconds remaining, and we were maybe 50 yards away, straight out by water from the dock. Then he turned sharply, aiming for a copse of maple trees near shore, just on the outside of the main fence. Muscles straining, veins in my pecs and biceps feeling about to burst, I got us around the corner from the blast zone as Brex gave the final countdown. "Five, four, three—"

Before he could finish, a brilliant flash like a bursting sun turned night into day.

Instinctively, I looked down at my feet to protect my night vision.

"That's odd," said Brex. "It detonated one point six seconds early. Good thing you—"

I couldn't hear the rest of his thought, because the ear-piercing sound of a two-thousand pound bomb going off shattered the atmosphere and shook the tree limbs high over our heads. A whirlwind of dust and debris headed our way, so I closed my eyes and dove face-down to the bottom of the boat. Brex did the same.

The wind howled like a tornado and splinters, twigs, and shards of metallic debris shrieked just overhead.

Then everything went quiet—or maybe I was just deafened. When I opened my eyes again and lifted my head a bit, I could see flickering flames and smoke in the distance.

"What was that thing? Some kind of mini-nuke?"

"Don't be absurd. Even I can't miniaturize a nuke to that extent. That would require having enough plutonium 239 or uranium 235 in at least two sub-critical masses, then enough high explosives to force the sub-critical masses together into a critical mass in which an uncontrolled chain reaction expels neutrons and converts all the mass into energy. The smallest possible nuke fills a backpack or a large briefcase."

"Not a good time for a science lecture, Brex."

"Sorry. Better row us back up there ASAP. We probably only have about two to five minutes before they scramble helicopters to send in reinforcements."

"So what do you call that thing, then?"

"I haven't made a final decision yet. My working name is Krakatoa."

I rowed us back, not quite so strenuously as when trying to save our lives. "That's a good one. A classic volcano. Go with that."

"Maybe. But there's been some other great volcanoes over the centuries, such as Vesuvius, which destroyed Pompei."

"Naw, Vesuvius sounds like a girlie statue, like the Venus de Milo in the Louvre. Krakatoa sounds scary and military and powerful. Stick with that."

There was nothing left of the main fence except some molten nubs lying along the scorched earth. Where the spiky fence had emerged, there was a vast crater about the size of a football field and up to ten or twelve feet deep in the center. As we hopped out of the boat among the remaining splinters of the pier, I could see within that crater the smoldering remains of the underground mechanism which had shot those spikes up only a few minutes ago.

On foot, we circled around the right edge of the crater towards the back patio of the palace. The bomb had shattered the upper swimming pool completely and ruptured the lower pool's base so that uncontrolled streams of water—water which had doubtless seen beautiful babes in bikinis splashing happily in recent weeks—poured down the hillside, washing the charred arms and legs and torsos of our foes towards the river, extinguishing the flickering remains of their burnt uniforms.

I looked past the patio towards the roof of the palace. All the searchlights were out. All the tall Corinthian columns along the back of the palace had fallen, as had the back wall and most of the roof along there.

I could see no living humans on the back lawn at all, nor on the patio. But as we approached the collapsed back of the palace itself, an enormous, multi-tiered paean to greed and pride and self-exaltation, made out of white stone and bedecked with hanging gardens, I could hear voices from within. It sounded not like someone in command giving orders, or troops responding in an organized fashion. Rather all I heard were groans and cries for help.

I pulled out my .45 as we cautiously entered the ruins of the back wall, the collapsed brick and stone and cedar paneling. I would give them help all right.

A quick bullet. That is, if any of them threatened us further.

Most of the interior lights along the back were out, but from further within the palace, light emanated from some rooms that still seemed relatively intact, though as we approached I could see extensive blast damage even deep within. Windows had been shattered, leaving glass everywhere. The blast had also toppled tables and chairs; broken dishes, vases, and art frames; torn off cabinets and closet doors; ripped open pipes, with water shooting out of fissures in all directions.

"I wonder where General Bnindagun is?"

"If you owned this palace and fancied yourself a king of the world, where would you be?"

"At the highest point, somewhere in the center so that I could be surrounded by guards and protection."

"Well, there you go."

Just then I saw a soldier lying under a pile of bricks from a collapsed fireplace, shakily raising his arm towards us, a pistol in his hand. I took him out with one shot to the head. "Brex, I'm nearly done on this mag, and who knows when a more serious fire fight might break out? You got another ace in that pouch for me just in case?"

"But of course!" He reached in his pouch and pulled out something resembling a primitive zip gun, the kind of gun even a gang kid in an inner city could make with a wood handle, lead pipe, a clothespin for a hammer, and a nail in said wood for a firing pin. I couldn't believe it.

"*That's* your second of three aces for me today?"

"I disguised it that way in case it gets lost. It's not really primitive." He handed it over.

Upon closer inspection I could see that the primitive features were 3-D laminate over a more sophisticated device underneath. I looked askance at him.

"Remember how Captain Kirk was always telling his space force to set phasers on stun? I always thought that was pretty stupid. You might need to stun one guy but shoot the next one dead a second later. Push this trigger to the left and it stuns; pull it to the right with your forefinger and it kills."

"So leftie leaves 'em loosie, but righty kills 'em tighty."

"I think that's it. No, wait, in all the excitement today I may have gotten that reversed."

"So left kills and right stuns?"

He looked flustered in the shadows of the ruined dining room we were walking through, what with candelabras from the table now embedded in nearby walls and fixtures. "No, wait, that's not right either. Just experiment on the next couple of guys and see what happens. You'll pick it up in no time."

"Wait, Captain Kirk? *Star Trek*? I used to watch that at my house after school and you'd be munching on Peanut M&Ms and poring over giant electronics and organic chemistry textbooks for post-graduate university programs."

"Absolutely. I never watched an episode, but while I was memorizing the periodic table of chemical elements and electronic circuits, I could still hear all the dialogue. I liked Spock but thought Kirk was a bit of a putz. Way too cute and casual with the crew for a real captain. Now that Picard, he was a different story—way more realistic and interesting."

"So you could follow the dialogue while memorizing advanced university textbooks in seventh grade?"

"Yep. I can multi-task, you know. Some girls can do that, but practically no males. But I can."

"And you are a model of modesty to us all."

"Yes, that is one of my best and most endearing qualities. I'm quite proud of it."

"I can see that."

Two creeps with raised pistols burst into the room, firing rapidly and adjusting the point of aim towards us.

I pushed the trigger left, and the first guy flew up into the air, crashed against the wall ten feet behind him, and fell to the floor with a cracked and bleeding skull, obviously dead.

I pulled the trigger right, and the second guy flew up into the air, crashed against a crumbling brick fireplace, and fell to the floor, obviously dead.

"Both ways kill, Brex. There's no either-or."

"You're doing it wrong, Jacks. Sometimes I forget I am dealing with a complete amateur who usually flubs up any advanced experimental weaponry."

Another enemy remained behind an open doorway and stuck just his gun arm into the room, firing blindly in our general direction. I flicked the trigger left at his arm and it flew back with such force that it propelled his entire body around in circles, exposing him fully to the second round, when I pulled right on the trigger. His body kept spinning and flew right up into the ceiling with such force that it impaled itself on the remaining shards of a broken chandelier overhead.

"Both settings are kill, Brex."

"Not when you're doing it right. Oh, what am I saying? You'll never get it right."

"Thanks, buddy. I appreciate your confidence."

"Just, mind you, don't again waste a second shot on any one gunsel. The battery has a limited life, you know. Remember that time boomerang in Mesopotamia? I don't have any spare batteries for this thing."

"I guess there's not room in that little waist-pack for everything."

"Right-o."

We had reached a spiral staircase in what I assumed was about the middle of the massive palace, but many of the marble tiles were cracked, some had chunks missing, and the steps were covered in broken glass and other debris. I motioned him to silence, then began to creep up the stairs, with him following closely.

I had counted thirteen cracked, unlucky steps when we reached the first landing. As we cautiously rounded the curve, wrapped around a giant cedar pillar decorated with gold leaf, I noted some odd portraits of the general at various stages of his life. Didn't major estates typically have art by the Great Masters of the past? Or portraits of one's lineage of ancestors? This guy was in all of the portraits. What an ego!

I saw one of him in civilian attire addressing the UN General Assembly, another of him in his military dress uniform being awarded his seventh star by what I assumed was the UN Secretary General, as the ceremony appeared to be within the UN sanctuary itself. Other portraits showed him on the grounds of New Eden riding a white stallion with his shirt off, looking very muscular and athletic; shooting skeet where the clay pigeons bore images of the faces of what I assumed were enemies of the state at that point; another of him holding a pistol and wearing an expression of righteous anger as he shot in the head at point blank range one of said state enemies. I could only assume it was a leader of the Waywards, a resistance leader brave to the last, with an expression of defiance on his face even as the bullet penetrated his skull while he stood manacled against a wall.

Then as we rounded the corner and started up the next flight of stairs, the portraits got even odder. One of him standing at an altar in his finest uniform surrounded by thousands of flowers of every size, color, and description, and a row of groomsmen also in their best military uniforms. *He got married? Who would marry a creep like that?*

Then I could pay attention to no more portraits, as seven bodyguards burst out of hiding places on the mezzanine floor, guns a-blazing. I fired the phaser and caught two with one blast, sending both in a cloud of dust back along the corridor, completely out of sight. With my left hand I pressed Brex against the pillar, signaling him to remain there as three more gunsels charged the top of the stairs from the left, right, and middle.

No time for me to fire thrice. In a flash of instinctual insight, I pressed the trigger once while panning the aim left to right, diluting the force of the power wave at any one point, but spreading it wide like a net, catching all three. But no single one got enough of the blast to die. Each lay thrashing on the floor, screaming in rage and pain.

I grabbed my .45 and used the remaining bullets of that first magazine to take out each in turn.

As the third of those breathed his last and relaxed in painless peace, the remaining two of the original group of seven jumped on me simultaneously. I was out of shells, with no time to reload either backup mag, and couldn't use the phaser without also hitting myself. Keeping both weapons in my hands as clubs, I went into martial arts mode, kicking, thrashing, blocking blows with my forearms, and clubbing at throats and heads with the weapons.

Those guys did not go down easily. They both rained blows on me simultaneously, and I began to lose focus as bursts of pain hit my neck, my kidneys, heart, and solar plexus, everywhere vital except between the legs. Somehow, I sensed each kick about to strike there and twisted at the last moment so that only my thigh muscles got pulverized.

No matter what I tried, though, I couldn't throw one off me long enough to fully attend to and dispatch the other.

Finally, as we hit and clawed in one single mass of tangled warriors, one conglomerate with three heads, six arms, and six legs, I deliberately shifted balance and pushed off the top stair, sending the human clump of us rolling and tossing down the stairs.

We landed at Brex's feet on the middle landing, all of us breathless and no doubt stunned and in pain. I knew I was. "Brexxie! Right leg... knife!"

He bent over, released the snap on the sheath, and retrieved my 13-inch fixed-blade Junglee Hattori fighter knife.

For a moment, too long a moment, I half-sensed, halfsaw him standing there, unsure what to do, as I struggled to breathe in the pulsating octopus of conglomerated bodies and one gunsel began chomping on my right forearm to make me drop the .45.

"Brexxie, carotids!"

He bent over and sliced the full length of the 7.75-inch MVS-8 steel blade across the neck of the one biting me. Pulses of blood shot up all over my chest, some even blind-

ing my eyes momentarily, but the force of the biting immediately subsided and within seconds ceased altogether.

I shrugged and twisted that body off the cluster while
Brexxie tried to get at the other man. But that one noted
the slashing blade and kept twisting me into position between him and Brex for protection.

I still held both weapons and now used them as a combined club to slam up into his chin from below, snapping
his head back and forcing his hold on me to let go. He stag-
gered backwards as I dropped the clubs, raised my hand,
and yelled to Brex, "Knife!"

He tossed it up and towards me so that the handle
would land in my palm. But my opponent saw the maneuver, leapt forward, pushed me out of the way with one
hand, and caught the knife with the other.

Before he could get into his knife-fighting crouch, I
rammed towards him, kicking with alternating legs at his
left foot as he moved it into position. With both hands I
chopped mercilessly again and again at the forearm holding
the knife. He kicked me with his good leg and rammed the
knife down towards my chest as I fell backwards.

I grabbed that wrist with both my hands and twisted as
we fell down the steps, so that he went down on his back,
head first, while I straddled him on top. I kept my left hand
on his knife wrist but used my right to grab him by the hair
and lift his head up until just the right moment, when we
approached a sharply cracked stair. Then I slammed his
head into the crack, hearing bones crunch and feeling the
damp ooze form on his scalp.

At the bottom of the stairs, his limbs all went limp, and
the knife fell to the floor. I grabbed the knife and stabbed it
all the way through his throat, from front to back. Then I
retrieved it, wiped it on his uniform, and rejoined Brex at
the middle landing.

He looked sick, but when I reached out to steady him,
he waved me away, handed me the dropped pistol and
phaser, and pointed upstairs.

Despite the racket we'd just made, we resumed our
stealthy creep up the stairs to the mezzanine and then all
the way to the top of the stairs with no further incident. On
the fourth floor we realized we'd reached what had to be the
master suite, just as I had imagined earlier.

Everything up there was ten times grander and glitzier than what we had seen before, a veritable Palace of Versailles, where King Louis XVI and his wife Marie Antoinette lived until the French Revolution. As we skulked down the corridor as quietly as possible, I noted features I had seen in a tourist trip to the original—the ornate tapestries along the walls, a gold rococo ceiling with real gold leaf forming intricate geometric patterns, a hall of mirrors, magnificent chandeliers in rows, one after another, and gold statuary set among potted plants.

And, of course, more portraits and photos of the general enjoying himself and showing off. In one he was dressed as a big game hunter and standing with a Winchester .458 magnum rifle over the dead body of a bull elephant with enormous ivory tusks. In another he stood alongside a pope at his apartment window in the Vatican, apparently making a joint address to the huge throng in St. Peter's Square below.

One in particular caught my attention. A group photo, it included Bnindagun and a future pope, and it looked as if taken on the same day as the one with the joint speech, but also with an older-looking Bouchard and someone I didn't recognize at all. "Brexxie, look at this one. Who's that fourth guy?"

He paused and looked very closely. "I'm not sure," he said, sounding perplexed. "It looks a lot like Roberto Alphonso Brindisi of Milan, who used to be the richest man in the world. But it can't be. He died a hundred years ago at least."

"Maybe one of his descendants, then. An heir to the family fortune."

"Maybe."

I heard a noise at the far end of the grand hall and began creeping forward again, noting yet more of the portraits portraying key events in the general's life.

One of him in a boxing ring, standing in triumph over a defeated opponent. Another hunting scene of him aiming his rifle at an attacking male lion. And several more of his wedding. One showed him at the altar with all his military groomsmen and bridesmaids all lined up amidst the glorious flowers.

Then we reached Bnindagun's equivalent of Versailles' *appartement du roi*, including the king's bedchamber. I wondered if this one had the same kind of four-poster bed with a ridiculously high upper tester from which flowed brocaded bed hangings, like I had seen when visiting Paris and its surrounding areas years before.

Before we could enter to check, I noted a tall figure standing just inside the doorway in his regal uniform with seven stars. And beside him, being held tightly by the shoulder with his left hand while his right aimed a pistol barrel at her head, stood a young lady who looked as if she could be the 14-year-old sister of my precious 6-year-old Little Sara.

The general leered at us "I thought I'd be running into you two sooner or later, in one space-time or another. That's why I've kept this little package handy ever since Bouchard told me you'd been snooping around our time train at the UN." Apparently, he had learned English since our previous encounter.

The girl looked at me plaintively. "Daddy, where have you been all this time? I missed you."

My heart sank to the floor.

22

Little Sara

The general started to move her towards the door, motioning with his pistol for us to step aside. "Here's what you're going to do. You're going to drop your weapons and let me get to the roof. An entire company of the 170th Special Operations Aviation Regiment should be arriving any second, led by my most trusted bodyguard and hero of the revolution, Captain Viktor Darebin. I suggest you leave while you still can. And maybe you'll live long enough to see Sara in another space and time."

I lowered my .45 and the experimental Star Trek phaser but did not drop them. I moved aside. Following my cue, Brex moved behind me.

"Smart boys. But if you want to live to see another day, you'd better start running. I can hear the rotary wings buzzing louder. You've probably got at most about half a minute head start."

I let them leave the room then grabbed Brex and looked earnestly into his face. "No more kidding around. Which way is 'stun'? I'm not letting that maniac take her, but I can't risk killing her."

"I swear, Jacks, I'm not farting around. I really don't remember. I designed it but never tested it before. Maybe you were right and both settings kill. There is no stun."

"What am I going to do?" I pleaded.

"Trust your warrior instincts. There comes a time when logic and science and facts can't control or even predict the outcome. Sometimes you gotta go with your gut."

"Well, where is that third ace you were talking about before? Is there another alternative to a bullet or a power wave?"

"Jacks, *you* are the third ace."

"I am? I thought I was the Jack. You were the king and we had three aces."

"You are the Jack in this hand, but also an ace. Sometimes you've gotta play two roles. You're a warrior. *Be* that warrior!"

My knees felt weak and my legs started to tremble as I raised the phaser and aimed at the general's feet. The power wave would hit her, too, but I prayed she'd survive. If I let him take her, I knew she wouldn't. Another few seconds, and they'd be beyond range, up the stairs, out of sight.

"Dad?" came Sara's voice. "Where are you taking me?"

"*Dad?*" I whispered in anguish, already sensing the answer.

Brex hissed, "Your surroundings, Jack! Note your surroundings."

I turned and scanned the room. The final of the series of wedding portraits. In this one I could see the maid of honor was Linda.

An eight-year-old Sara was the flower girl.

And the bride was... was my Momma Sara.

I stopped breathing and turned toward the shrinking figure of the general as he headed towards the stairs to the roof. "Sara? He married my *Sara?*"

"No, idiot... Tara. Didn't you notice the scar on the left earlobe?"

I raised the phaser. My finger started to push left, then I blinked and shook my head and started to pull right. My eyes were watering and I blinked furiously, trying to see.

"Do it!" hissed Brex. "*Shoot!*"

I pulled all the way to the left, expecting to see both of them fly off their feet and bounce into the far wall. I hoped Bnindagun's carcass would help cushion Sara's impact.

Nothing.

Frantically I pushed and pulled the trigger.

Nothing. "Battery's dead," I moaned, tossing the piece of crap on the floor and tightening the grip on my Colt. As I headed up the stairs, about a dozen paces behind them, I replaced the empty mag of my .45 with a fresh one. I could hear Brex's footfalls on the steps behind me as I reached the top.

The exit door to the roof was closing just as I surged forward and threw it open again. I could see the helipad marked with a single giant X. Just room for one helicopter to land, and the general and Sara were headed towards that spot as the whirlybird rapidly descended. The remaining helicopters hovered in the air, but from one over each end of the roof, dozens of aviation special forces troops were rappelling down in full battle gear.

I grabbed Brex and propelled him forward with me at twice his normal speed.

The moment the first helicopter made contact with the X landing spot, Bnindagun threw open the door and tossed Sara inside.

At that moment, I fired three times into the back of his skull, sending brains and blood and skull fragments along the side of the chopper. Sara screamed and recoiled in horror.

I ran to the open door, and before they could move, I took out the pilot and co-pilot, each with one head shot.

As Brex breathlessly caught up with me, I kicked the general's lifeless body over and fired my final two shots of the mag, one in the center of his throat and one into his chest where his heart should be. If he had one. I climbed in and tossed the other two bodies out to the roof as Brex scampered aboard, trying to stay out of the way.

"Do you know how to fly this thing?" he asked.

"No idea. Do you?"

"Well, I've never tried, but I read a technical manual on it once while I was waiting in the dentist's office for my appointment. I think I can do it. It looks pretty easy—just a matter of keeping a balance between the cyclic and the collective controls."

"Be my guest."

As he got into the pilot's seat and started fiddling with the controls, I exchanged into my last fresh magazine and fired at the lead assault trooper in each of the two columns heading our way from two different directions. Each went down. "Move it, buddy! Get us up!"

He must have been doing something right, because the engine whined louder and the blade rotation picked up, kicking a powerful wind into the faces of the approaching troops, forcing them to slow down. I fired at the remaining leader in each of the approaching columns, and they dropped. The third man in each line went into a crouch and waved for his troops to fan out.

The chopper lifted a few feet, shook and shimmied and nearly tipped over, and bounced back down to the big X.

"It's tougher than I thought," said Brex. "I know what to do, but getting the balance just right takes a bit of practice. Like the first time you ride a two-wheel bike."

"Just make it so."

"Yes, sir, Captain Picard."

Suddenly the chopper flew straight up with such velocity I thought I'd upchuck the canapes from the UN cocktail party.

"Got it!" yelled Brex over the whine of the engine.

"Way to go, buddy!"

The troops below began to fire at us, but within a second or two, Brex had veered over the surrounding trees and kept low. Rifle fire from the roof couldn't hit us there. But now four helicopters already in the air followed in swift pursuit.

"Do you know how to fire those missiles?" I asked Brex.

"No idea. That wasn't in the TM I read."

"I don't either. But I can sure work this M60 door gun." I maneuvered it into position in the still open doorway and yelled to Sara to buckle in and then cover her ears. She did.

I didn't want to kill these guys. Some might not have been true believers in the global plot to destroy America and take over the world, but just decent grunts doing their job and trying to feed their families. Anything but become one of the masses with nothing, no future at all in the new utopia. So instead of shooting to kill, I tried to damage the rotary blades of the two lead choppers so that they would be forced to land.

I heard the roar of the weapon and saw sparks as bullets struck the rotary wings, which then whined and emitted smoke, and soon those two went into rapid descent mode. The pilots in the two choppers behind them quickly caught on to my maneuver and began to fly in random zig-zag patterns as they held back and likely prepared to fire something at us.

Suddenly I saw two flashes of flame from the missile tubes mounted under the door gun swivel support, and two AIM-92 Stinger air-to-air missiles streaked through the sky in our direction.

"Evasive action, Brex!" I shouted.

My stomach rose to my throat as Brex went into a steep dive, barely skirted the treetops along the river bank, then swooped low, almost to the water's surface, then did a 180 so the engine exhaust signature the missiles were honed onto would be in the other direction.

Miraculously, it worked, and both missiles slammed into the water before exploding, now about a hundred yards behind us.

Brex lifted us up again and we were facing the two remaining choppers. I let go of the M60 and clambered into the co-pilot's seat, examined the missile controls quickly, and started pressing buttons more or less randomly.

Well, not entirely randomly. I could tell the difference between the UNLOCK button and the FIRE button, but I wasn't sure about how to aim. Regardless, the missiles below us all shot out in rapid sequence in the general direction of our foes. They went into evasive action, delaying their pursuit, and soon we were at maximum forward airspeed beyond their range.

"Where are we headed, Brexxie?" I asked.

"The UN HQ. It's only a couple of miles from here."

"Headed for the time train?"

"Yep. That's our only hope of getting back to our home and time and maybe undoing this dreadful space-time sequence we've seen here today."

I turned back to reassure Sara, intending to say, *You hear that, baby? We're going home.* But while I had eyes directly on her and had started speaking, she suddenly vanished.

I gasped. "Brexxie, Sara just completely disappeared while I was looking right at her!"

"Then I guess we succeeded," he said simply. "We ended up erasing this potential timeline."

23

Bouchard

Within moments we were over the East River in the vicinity of the UN compound, and Brexxie slowed and began to descend towards the little grassy area at the north end of the compound, where we had seen the Schimmerplotz as the general's Ubaidian troops swarmed out of Mesopotamia into the New York City of our day.

He grabbed the radio, flipped a switch, and proclaimed, "Mayday! Mayday! We have sustained major damage and must make an emergency landing. Request permission to land." Without waiting for a response, he proceeded to do so.

"Wait a sec, Brexxie. I thought this was considered foreign territory and not part of America. Can we do this without getting shot down?"

"It is extraterritorial, but at least in our day they didn't have their own army and air force, etc. They had an agreement with the city to use regular municipal police, firefighters, and so on in exchange for the right to enter their territorial space when needed."

"So where is their stop on the time subway, do you think?"

"The one Sara and I saw in Mesopotamia was controlled underneath the ziggurat, their most important building at that time, so I'm guessing the one here is controlled from beneath *their* most important."

"Namely the landmark thirty-nine-story Secretariat Building, near where we last saw the delightful Delegate Bouchard?"

"Nice thinking, Jacks. You've caught up with me without me having to explain everything to you. Kinda like the family dog when he sees the dad grab the car keys and head for the garage door. He's ready to go, too."

"Woof, woof."

Brex lowered the collective control with his left hand and we went down in the middle of the grassy space. A little too fast, but it wasn't that unpleasant a landing. Just a bit of a bump. Then he cut the engine and let the rotation of the wings die down.

He hopped out. "Let's go, boy," he said in a tone usually reserved for addressing BigBear.

I woofed again as I hopped out. "Okay, take me to Petco, but let's skip the vet. I'm rather partial to keeping my anatomy intact."

He snickered. "In that case, you'd better bring a weapon."

"My .45 and all its mags are empty. But I can unhook that M60 machine gun and carry it."

"Naw, that's too obvious. They'd know we were trouble if we walked away like that."

"I still have my Hattori fighter knife."

"Good. Yeah, keep that in its sheath."

"And my Smith and Wesson Special Ops folder. You want that?"

"Naw, let me see if there's anything in the chopper." He looked back in and pulled something off a mount on the inside of the door. "A flare gun. One shot, but it might be useful." He struggled to find someplace to hide it, but it was too large for his tiny frame and light clothing.

"Here," I said, "let me carry it." He handed it over, and I stuck it under the waistband in the small of my back, underneath the shirt.

Just then, a security detail of three guards approached. The leading one stopped barely out of arm's reach. "Are you gentlemen okay?"

"No injuries," I reported.

"Any danger of fire? Should we call the NYFD?"

"That wasn't the problem," said Brex. "It was a mechanical malfunction in the controls."

"Well, come to my office, and you can call your HQ to send in a retrieval unit to pick you up."

"Wait," said Brex. "We actually needed to come here in the first place. We have a message from General Bnindagun for Delegate Bouchard."

"*Delegate?*" He suddenly looked suspicious. "You mean secretary general?"

Brex and I exchanged knowing glances.

But so did the security chief and his two men. All of them kept their hands near their sidearms. Turning back to us, the chief said, "You two better come with us. I have to file a report with the secretary general's office and see what they want to do with you."

"We have an urgent message from the general for Secretary Bouchard personally. We just left New Eden and spoke with General Bnindagun no more than five or six minutes ago."

"You are definitely not attired like his usual emissaries. I've got to check this out."

"This is an emergency situation," Brex said. "We didn't have time to get dressed up as usual."

Turning to his men, the security leader said, "Escort these two to the secretary general's office. I'm going to radio ahead and confirm what they want to do."

"This way, gentlemen," one of them said.

By the time we reached the office, another half dozen guards had assembled there. One of Bouchard's assistants intercepted us. "Exactly who are you two? We have just received reports of an assault on the New Eden compound."

"I know," said Brex. "We were there when it happened. We were the last to speak with General Bnindagun, and we have an urgent message from him for Secretary General Bouchard."

"Something is not right with your story. We were told by the 170th SOAR commander on site that two outsiders matching your description made off with one of their assault helicopters, the very one you just landed on our north lawn."

"Exactly," said Brex. "He sent us here."

"This doesn't make sense at all." He raised a finger, and all guards drew their weapons and kept wary eyes on us. "Now tell me who you two are."

"I'm Breslin Herndon, the general's senior science advisor, and this is Major Jack Rigalto, chief of the general's security detail. And I advise you in the strongest possible terms to allow us to complete our mission... or you will be facing the general's wrath—and I'm sure you know what *that* is like!"

Brex tried to look tough and scary, but with his tiny size, it was not so much how he looked but what he said that alarmed the assistant, and he paled. "Tell me your message right now, and I will immediately convey it to Secretary Bouchard."

"The very unit that is reporting to you about the assault on the New Eden compound is the one doing it! This is a coup attempt by the 170th, and they have destroyed most of the compound. Walls are down, nearly all of the general's security men have been shot, and bodies lie scattered everywhere, inside the main building and all along the back as far as the river. Even the pool was bombed and utterly destroyed."

"Not the two-tiered pool? That was beautiful, a wonderful place to relax at one of their parties."

"Yes, the pool. And you'll never be invited to another party up there unless you get moving *toute de suite*. We have to stop this coup attempt and save Bnindagun before it is too late. Believe *nothing* you hear from the 170th people. That's all propaganda meant to delay our response until it is too late. You must issue warnings at once to all forces loyal to the general to believe nothing from the 170th until their leaders can be apprehended and forced to confess! *Comprenez vous?*"

"*Oui!*" He turned and dashed from the room.

A nervous-looking Bouchard stumbled out to meet us within moments. "You two again? What are you doing here?"

"After seeing you that night at the cocktail party years ago, we reconsidered your offer and General Bnindagun convinced us to join his secret group of inside advisors."

"He never told me that. And why haven't I seen you before at any of our planning meetings?"

"Like I said, we are on the secret team. You know how the general holds things together by keeping his different factions separate from each other and often unaware of what the others are doing?"

"That's true," he mused. "But we still have reports that you two are behind the assault today."

"Apply a little logic, Bouchard. How could two unarmed men accomplish all that? And who has a fleet of assault choppers firing missiles and dropping bombs on New Eden right now as we speak? Which is the more likely culprit?"

"Yes, but—"

"There is no *but*, just the urgency of acting at once. Delaying your response to aid your leader in the face of a coup attempt is treason! Do you want the general to see you as a traitor?"

"*Mon Dieu!*"

"I can prove to you that we've been on his secret team all these years. We know every inch of the grounds and every room in the New Eden palace, where we've lived for years. Ask me three questions, and if I don't know the answers, then doubt me. But believe nothing you hear from the 170th people. Why do you think we are here reporting to you in person and they are attacking the general and spreading propaganda and lies from a safe distance?"

Bouchard looked shaky, but still unsatisfied. "Three questions, then, so I know you are for real. How many floors in the center of the Palace?"

"Four," Brex responded.

"What do you see on walls of the central spiral staircase and his private apartments?"

"Portraits of the general at his wedding, making a joint address with the pope, hunting elephants, and proving to the people his many heroic qualities."

"What are his private apartments modeled after?"

I answered that one. "The Palace of Versailles, just outside Paris. All the way down to the gold rococo ceiling and even a giant four-poster bed like Louis XVI's."

"Really? Even I have never been as far as his actual bedroom."

"Easily explained. I'm the chief of his secret security force. I have to know everything."

"But he married what I thought was your widow! And adopted your child!"

"We sacrifice what we must for our dear leader in order to create a perfect world."

"Understood." Bouchard turned to his guards. "I'm still not sure whether to trust these two, but we can't hesitate to help the general. I myself have seen recent intel reports suggesting a coup attempt may be in the works." Turning to us, he said, "What does the general want me to do?"

Brex didn't bat an eye. "The situation is dire and he is running out of time. We have to adjust the time controls so he can bring in more reinforcements he knows he can trust. Take us to the control room at once."

24

The Control Room

Two guards came along as Bouchard and his assistant led us to the secretary general's private elevator, and we descended all the way to the basement. There the elevator stopped, but no doors opened. Both senior men produced keys and inserted each into a different lock at opposite ends of the elevator, turning them at precisely the same moment, and finally the door opened.

The two guards stayed in the open elevator.

The rest of us entered a weirdly lit room resembling a laboratory with all glass walls and observation cameras in every corner. I could see a pair of gas nozzles in the ceiling, and assumed they were available to fill the room with knockout—or perhaps lethal—gas if desired by someone in an observation room somewhere who saw anything amiss.

The two men drew out different keys this time, and again went to locks in two different corners of the far wall and synchronized their release.

We passed into a control area beyond, which looked just like an entrance to a subway, except for the presence of only minimal stairs down.

"What setting does the general need?" asked Bouchard.

"Take us back to the morning after that cocktail party where we first met you face to face."

Brouchard's face scrunched up. "How could that possibly help the general now?" Brex had no quick answer, and

Bouchard's expression changed in an instant. "Oh, no, I fell for your lies. Guards!"

I threw the assistant into the approaching men, knocking them all down in the gas antechamber. Then I kicked the door shut between them and us three in the control room.

"The general will kill me if I help you."

"I'll kill you if you don't." I pulled out the flare gun from the chopper and released the safety, aiming it squarely into his chest. "And then I'll destroy this entire control room so that you can never use it again."

"No, wait. I'll do what you ask. You two get into the conveyer and I'll send you wherever you want."

"And land in some active volcano or a dinosaur nest with new hatchlings? Fat chance," I said, grabbing his shoulder. "No. You're coming with us."

Brex was examining the controls, his nose an inch from the panel.

"Can you set it, Brexxie?"

"I'm not sure. I think the labels are in a written form of Origanis, which would be a modern adaptation as I'm pretty sure there was no written form in the days that this was spoken among all mankind."

"How could you possibly know that?" asked the dumbfounded Bouchard.

"Like I said, I'm the senior science advisor."

"Wait a second, Brexxie," I said. "Can you set the controls and jump in with us?"

"Tough luck, guys." Bouchard hooted. "Your master plan is falling apart. One of you has got to stay here."

I raised my palm to slap him, but then thought better of it. Instead I grabbed him by the collar and bent low into his personal space. "No, *your* master plan is falling apart. You'll never subjugate the entire world as long as there is one patriot willing to fight for freedom."

"Which is exactly why we kill you off everywhere and every time we can find you!" he spat right back.

I heard beating on the glass walls of the antechamber, and saw the two guards and the assistant frantically pounding on the glass as their space filled up with toxic gas.

I looked at my buddy. "Brex, set it and show me the button to push. I'll stay here, and you go back with him."

He fiddled with the controls, turning dials, flipping levers, and opening the fail-safe lids on some buttons. "Don't be an idiot, Jacks. You can't handle this, and I can't handle him. You've got to go, and I've got to stay."

Something welled up from deep inside me, and I tried to hold it in. "Brex, I can't leave you like this. We'll find some other way."

"There *is* no other way. And you know it! You've got to think of the team, step over the body of your fallen comrade, close ranks with the others, and proceed with your mission. Only you can stop them now and save Linda, and Sara, and Sara, and all the rest. Just tell Linda I love her!"

"No, Brex, wait!"

But it was too late. He pressed the final button, and in a moment, Bouchard and I entered the void.

25

Two Bouchards

In a flash we found ourselves on the pavement outside Linda's condominium building next to the East River—daylight now, rather than late at night after the UN cocktail party.

Brexxie certainly got the location right, and I hoped he had the timing right, too. I didn't particularly want to find myself in a year before I had married or after Sara had grown up. I didn't want to miss my life as I knew it.

"Now what?" asked Bouchard sullenly.

"Listen, Bouchard. You know my word is good. I don't spend all my time lying and deceiving like you guys do. If you cooperate, I swear I won't kill you. With your talents and connections, you'll do fine in an environment like this."

"What if I refuse?"

"We'll probably both die, but I'll make sure you do first."

"So what do you want me to do?"

"We've got to get back to your office and use the controls there to try and bring Brexxie back."

"Can't. Impossible."

"What do you mean?"

"I can't co-exist as my future and present selves in the same place. If we go to my office, one or both of myselves will vanish instantly. We learned that one the hard way. It was a problem none of us could solve."

"Would you rather vanish right now or give it a chance and find out? Maybe you'll both work together as friends, like twin brothers or something."

"That's an interesting notion, coming from an idiot musclehead like you, but completely impossible. For one thing, the future me, the current me, would remember that if it had happened, and I sure don't."

"Well, let's find out. You may still have a long and prosperous life in this timeline on your own... if you cooperate."

I hailed a cab and we both got in. A crumpled, discarded newspaper lay on the seat and I glanced at the date. Brexxie got us back on the right day. Now it was all up to me.

I told the cabbie to take us to the UN, then turned to Bouchard in the seat beside me. "There's something I just can't understand about you, *Frère Jacques* Bouchard. Why do you so loathe and despise patriotic Americans who love and want to preserve their country and way of life?"

"You really want to get into this? Now?"

Our driver sped along, deftly bobbing and weaving in the heavy traffic and quickly departing lanes blocked ahead by delivery trucks pausing for drop-offs.

"Yes, I don't understand why you guys feel you must conquer and control us and dictate every thought we are allowed to have. Why can't it ever just be live and let live? We don't feel we must have totalitarian control over you, but you spend all your time trying to force your totalitarian views and plans on us."

"The fact that you are so blind to dialectical materialism, the inevitable triumph of communism, our coming creation of the perfect man, and the utter need to crush the American system and fundamentally transform this country just goes to prove you have had nothing but a jingoistic upbringing and been brainwashed by your patriarchal, racist society. You are part of the dying past; we are the vanguard of the future."

Out of the corner of my eye I could see an old lady with a small terrier on a leash suddenly appear around the front of a double-parked truck. Our driver slammed on the brakes just in time to avoid a collision.

"You're just spouting the same old Marxist ideology and clichés and bullcrap I've heard all my life. And not one single word of it makes any sense or can hold up under the slightest scrutiny. You think you are such a visionary, but you have blinded yourself to any and all facets of reality which don't comport with your preconceptions."

"You're insane!" spat Bouchard.

"No, *you* are. The very definition of insanity is doing the same thing over and over again and yet expecting the results to come out differently. Nothing but horror, suffering, death, and destruction after you leftists took over Russia, then China, Cuba, Southeast Asia, Venezuela, countless countries in Africa, and on and on. Just an endless parade of human misery."

The woman in the street was slow to move, so our driver honked three times to wake her up. The dog barked at us, but the woman tugged his leash and they managed to cross the street without getting mangled. We started moving again.

Bouchard's face turned red. "The system you so treasure is inherently violent and racist and destructive to the environment and world peace."

"No," I said. "Systems—or society at large—are not what corrupt individuals. The fact that individuals are inherently corrupt to begin with leads to flawed, imperfect systems. You have everything exactly backward, and any system you posit based on nothing but flawed and erroneous presuppositions will inevitably and invariably backfire and turn out wrong. Garbage in; garbage out."

Our driver honked again, really leaning on the horn this time, as a previously double-parked truck pulled out right in front of us.

"Your systems and superstitious beliefs are dying. We will bury you, to use the immortal words of Khruschev, and usher in a global utopia of perfection and peace."

"Complete nonsense, and everything you think, do, and say, every moment of the day, proves you are wrong and that I am right."

"No, once we eliminate all you racist, sexist, jingoistic irredeemable Waywards, the world will finally experience perfect peace, tranquility, and social justice for all. No more inequality nor war."

We arrived at our stop, and I paid the driver. "You know what, Bouchard? I don't think you even really believe the nonstop nonsense you keep spouting. That's really all just a rationalization for your lust to power. You deceive the masses, especially the young who aren't mature enough yet to think for themselves, and you may try to deceive even yourself, but you know deep in your heart of hearts what you really plan to do."

"And what is that, you capitalist idiot?"

I looked at him and repressed my desire to stomp him like a bug. "You preach peace, but plan to torture and murder everyone who disagrees with you. You preach equality, but dismiss the masses as unworthy of even basic human rights while you plan to live like an emperor at their expense. You preach tolerance, but haven't the slightest degree of tolerance towards anyone who disagrees with you. Your entire life is a self-contradictory web of lies and deceptions in every last detail. Everything you say is just a mask to hide your despicable lust for absolute power over others."

"Go jump in the Euphrates!"

The sun was bright after we left the cab, but soon we passed under the shade of the towering Secretariat Building. I kept a wary eye on the pedestrians walking around us. "No, one last comment and then I'll shut up and leave you with your self-delusions until the day you meet your Maker and all delusions will be shed and you will see yourself for what you truly are."

"More superstitious rambling, the opiate of the masses."

A man began to eye us, and I wondered if he were an undercover guard or an agent. I kept close to Bouchard as we walked so he wouldn't be able to bolt away without me knocking him down first. "It was bad enough when I first met you, eight years ago in your timeline, for you to spout obvious nonsense about the glories of socialism, but you went on to actually do exactly what all socialists have always done and always will do. I saw your 'New Eden.' You promised a paradise but produced nothing but a den of misery for all but the most powerful elite at the very pinnacle of your society. So much for justice, tolerance, peace, and equality."

"Shut up! I'm tired of listening to your backwards philosophy."

I shrugged. "Lead the way to your time controls, then. I assume the location is the same as we just experienced?"

"Yes. But if you weren't just a musclehead, you'd recall I couldn't go down there by myself. It requires two different people with two different keys, standing at least a dozen feet apart, but acting in perfect synchrony."

"Well, get me the other key and I'll play number two."

"You look like a big pile of Number Two, so that fits!"

The man who had eyed us kept walking, but I wondered if we'd see him again. "You're a funny guy, *Frère Jacques*! But your standup gig is over. How do we get that key?"

"We don't. When you kidnapped me, in that timeline, I was secretary general. I ran the whole UN. I had control over all the other keys. But you've taken us back to the time when I was still just a lowly delegate within one single nation's delegation, a good half-dozen steps lower down the totem pole."

I paused at the entrance, where people poured in and out of the busy building. "Nice try, but I know even then, which is to say right now, you were—are—working directly for Mr. Big, whoever he is. You weren't really working for the government of Canada or for the good of your own fellow citizens. You were at the highest level of the globalist plot, directly under its mastermind. Now get me that other key!"

"Impossible!"

"Let's go to your office, then. I'll bet it's there. If not, it must be with your fellow-conspirator from Germany or the one from France."

Within minutes, we entered the antechamber for his office, and the secretary sitting at the front desk looked startled. "Sir? I thought you were in your office! How did you leave without me noticing?"

He said nothing, but just waved at her, a curious little wave with his hand down low, at waist level rather than chest level. *Must be a sign of their familiarity. Perhaps she's his lover.*

He strode right up to the door, opened it, and then vanished into thin air before he could enter. And as the Bouchard of my day looked startled and rose up from his desk to confront me, I could hear the alarm that the secretary had apparently set off at the other Bouchard's special signal.

And I could hear the rapid footsteps of security forces racing our way.

Trapped!

26

Between a Rock and a Hard Place

"Arrest him and cuff him to that chair," Bouchard barked.

I saw nothing to gain at that point by resisting, for I as yet had neither of the keys required to get Brexxie back. I let them cuff me.

Bouchard perched on top of his desk, some six feet away, and glowered at me as I sat in restraints with a guard on either side and one at my back. "What in blazes are you doing back here? You are trespassing on foreign soil. Last night I explicitly informed you that you were unwelcome here."

"I'm not the man you spoke with last night," I said.

He guffawed. "Really? Well, you look a lot like him."

"Are you sure you want to get into this right now? With so many ears present? I have a special message for you with some... *futuristic* impact." I used my most ominous, low tone of voice on that word.

He paused, then glanced up at the security folks. "You two leave. Alain stays." After the door closed, he turned back to me. "I'm listening."

"Did you see who brought me here?"

"No. I just saw you."

"Then ask your secretary who brought me here."

169

He called her in, and she planted her hands on her hips. "Sir, do you have a twin brother or something? I thought it was you. But I also thought you were still in the office. I'm very confused."

"Thank you, Angelique. It has been a rough morning. Why don't you go take an extended coffee break until you feel better again?"

"Thank you, sir."

After the door closed behind her, he turned back to me. "So—?"

"Jacques Bouchard, you brought me here. The future you, that is."

He blinked.

"Are you sure you want Alain to hear the rest of this?"

"Yes. He's my most trusted associate. Go ahead."

"All of our plans with the general go just fine from this day forward—"

"Good. Good. Wait, you said *our*?"

"Affirmative. Breslin Herndon and I joined your team a short while after our visit to your cocktail party last night."

"That's fine. That's what we wanted. I figured you guys would wise up and join the winning team. Why go down with the ship when you can enjoy the tropical island with all its riches and pretty women and—"

"And power. Don't forget power."

"Of course. That's what drives us all. So what went—I mean, *goes* wrong with our master plan?"

"Well, the first part went perfectly, of course. We were able to throw open every border in the world and bring a billion warriors from the so-called lost cultures of the past directly into first world countries of the present."

"So now you know the secret behind all the past cultures which, according to most historians, mysteriously disappeared."

"Yes. And the second step worked perfectly, too."

"You mean ripping the weapons out of the cold, dead hands of those idiots still clinging to notions of patriotism to long-dead nations?"

"Obviously."

"So what went wrong?" Jacques looked genuinely puzzled.

*How can anything ever go wrong for the left? They al-
ways get anything and everything they want on this temporal plane. They control everything, education, news, art,
film, TV, all the mainstream media, all the political culture.*

"Nothing at first. We sowed chaos, promised salvation
to the terrified masses if they would only turn over all their
freedoms and rights to us, then murdered them by the
hundreds of millions as soon as we took absolute power."

"Fine. Yes, that's the plan. So—?"

"Oh, and you get the reward you were promised. You
personally take charge of the entire UN. And General
Bnindagun becomes commander-in-chief of the combined
world army."

"Good. This is all very good news. So we reap the re-
wards we were promised. I'm not seeing a problem yet."

"Factionalism. The Global Unity Party begins to split
and the different factions turn on each other, like Stalin
having his former ally Trotsky assassinated. Specifically,
Herndon and I were with the general when backup security
forces attacked his personal bodyguard and destroyed his
palace. Herndon is waiting there, but you and I need to
bring him here to ensure those coup leaders of the future
never rise to positions of power and authority now."

"Wait a second. How do I know you are really from the
future?"

"That's very easy to prove. You and I came back just a
few minutes ago, but Herndon's still there with the list of
traitors to be prevented. To prove I know where it is, I will
take you to the time train control room. You will locate
Herndon in the future, which proves I was also there, because I'll give you the location and date, and we'll retrieve
him and the list. The fact that you brought me here proves
the future you is working with us."

"That makes sense, but I'm going to have to run this by
the boss."

The boss. I had to think fast. Brexxie frequently admon-
ished me to pay attention to my surroundings, to pull the
secrets from the walls themselves. I looked quickly at the
walls in this room. There was a photo of Bouchard with the
same man I had noted with him and two others in that New
Eden portrait. The man Brexxie said looked like the long-
dead Roberto Alphonso Brindisi, once the richest man in

the world. *Was the man in that New Eden portrait and the photo here the same person, traveling through time, or was it an heir to a family fortune amassed over the centuries, perhaps over the millenia?*

What was it Sara had said repeatedly, follow the money? Who would profit the most from a global empire? *Wouldn't it be the wealthy person or family who had funded it to start with?*

I myself in Mesopotamia had noted the poor foot health of the Ubaidians and figured anyone who had a solution to that problem could readily become the owner of all the wealth around. Was there someone else, even way back there at the original time of Bnindagun, who had risen to prominence and wealth by solving—or at least promising to solve—some other problem of the people?

Was there a long familial line straight from the one-world, one-language, pre-Babel people who had persisted all these thousands of years and were now in our time trying at last to become globalist gods ruling over the rest of humanity with absolute power? Or was it the same original man traveling through time?

There were no choices left. I had to take the chance.

I turned to Bouchard. "I know who you are going to call, which is more proof that I have come from your future."

"Coming from the future would be the only possible way you would know. That's the best-kept secret of our group up to this point."

"It's Brindisi."

Bouchard let out a low whistle. "Wow. You've proven yourself, all right, Mr. Rigalto. But I still don't trust your motives, allegiance, and intentions. Alain, release his cuffs, but keep a close eye—and weapon—trained on him. We've got a list to retrieve, but I want to make sure *we* get to use it, not him."

27
Reunited

I'll never forget that feeling of relief as I stood there in the current-day control room, watched Bouchard fiddle with some controls, and then saw Brexxie materialize in the conveyor.

At first, he looked surprised. But before he could reveal his astonishment and give away the game...

"Welcome back, Brexxie!" I knew my smile had to be goofy and too big, but I couldn't help it.

He smiled broadly, too. "So you missed me, buddy? I knew it." He glanced at Bouchard and Alain as he walked over and patted me on the back.

"Nah, just proceeding with the mission. The future Bouchard who came back with me this morning vanished when we went to tell the current Mr. B how General Bnindagun sent us all back to prevent the coup attempt you and I witnessed at New Eden. He's ready for your list of future traitors we can work together to eliminate now."

"Yeah, right. Got it." He turned to Bouchard. "We need to start with your inside man in our old agency, the Cosmic Intelligence Group. The one who tipped you off when I reported our first Schimmerplotz encounter."

"You mean Assistant Director Addams?"

"That's the one."

"Who else?"

"The company commander of the 170th SOAR unit for backup New Eden security."

"What's his name?"

"Darebin. Viktor Darebin. He's a captain then, but must in this day have a lower rank."

"We'll check it out. Anyone else?"

"Of course. All Darebin's revolutionary associates now and future lieutenants then. We don't have all their names, but he knows them. I'm sure you can persuade him to talk."

Bouchard clicked his tongue. "Bnindagun has ways to make the stones of the desert sing, believe me."

"Anything else?" Brex asked.

I patted my stomach "Well, I'm starved. In my timeline, I haven't eaten a thing since being with the general in the coup attempt and rushing back here to prevent it all."

Bouchard glanced at the wall clock, "The UN Delegates Dining Room is open and has a remarkable three-course international lunch. We could go there."

"I've read about that. *Prix-fixe*, right?"

"Yes, but you would, of course, be my guests *gratis*."

Brex looked amused. "That's the same dining hall as for the cocktail party last night, isn't it?"

"Why, yes, yes, it is."

"I like the symbolism of that, Mr. Bouchard. We got off to a bad start last night, but we can start anew today. Do you mind if we invite the ladies as well?"

"Not at all. The restaurant menu changes every single day, but there are always wonderful international specialties. I happened to glance online at the menu for today, and they're having items like baby kale salad, duo duck confit with forbidden rice, and raspberry mousse cake."

"Forbidden rice?" I asked.

Brex laughed. "It's a low calorie, high-antioxidant black rice that used to be forbidden to anyone in China except the emperor. Very healthy."

"I believe you are correct. It has a heckuva lot more flavor, too. I love it."

"No Peanut M&Ms?" asked Brex with a hint of disappointment in his voice.

"What?" asked Bouchard.

"It's nothing." I shushed Brex. "Later, buddy, later. We'll find you some."

As we walked over to the UN Conference Building, Brex beamed at me. "I knew it. I told you we were best friends. You dropped everything else and came back for me first."

I started to chide him, but the words wouldn't come out of my open mouth. Instead I just sighed and shook my head.

"Come on, admit it. I'm your BFF, right?"

I shrugged, finally finding my voice. "Brex, you know taking care of you is my job. CIG hired me to save your sorry anatomy every time you get in trouble, which you are so very prone to do, and I am darn good at my job."

"It's more than just a job for you, and you know it." He didn't sound miffed; he was still smiling from ear to ear.

"Brexxie, we're partners, and a real man never abandons his partner, not while there's still a chance he's alive. That's just Basic Guy Code one-oh-one."

Nothing dampened his enthusiasm. "Don't worry. I won't tell anyone. I won't blow your cover as an alpha, macho, silverback gorilla. Your secret is safe with me."

I relented and grinned. "And, of course, we're friends, dude! Do you want just the words or should I punch you, too?" My right fist clenched involuntarily, and I started to raise my right arm.

Brex took a step to the side. "Words are enough for me, Jacks. The less punching, the better."

"Okay, but generally, I am better with punches than words." I relaxed my arm again.

"Yeah, I've noticed. Listen, I know your dad was a swell guy, a great husband and father, a good provider, but he was just too macho himself to teach you how to express emotions verbally. He would wrestle with you, pick you up and throw you on the bed, grab you around the neck and rub your head with his knuckles in a playful way. He loved you, but that was the only way he could show it. I understand. I don't blame him; he was raised that way himself. But you gotta realize not everyone is raised like that—"

"Brex! I swear if you don't shut up right now, I'm gonna—"

"Tut!" he croaked, then smiled at me as he pretended to air-zip his lips shut with his fingers.

As we kept walking, I called Sara on my cell phone.

"You're back already? I was so worried last night. Is everything okay?"

"I think so. Is Linda with you?"

"Yes. I brought her up to date after you two disappeared, and she was happy to come home with me."

"How would you like to come to the UN Delegates Dining Room for lunch today?"

"Are you kidding me? Isn't that where we got kicked out last night?"

"Yeah, but a lot has changed since then. I can't tell you about it now, but this is our chance to find out more about what's going on."

"Are you freaking kidding me? It's a trap! Get out of there right now, while you still can."

A menacing voice spoke from a few paces behind us. "Too late."

I turned. Alain, the other two guards who had apprehended me before, and the undercover agent who first noted me at the entrance now stood with guns drawn and pointed at the two of us.

Before either of us could say anything, Alain motioned with his head. "This way. Masquerade is over. Mr. Brindisi wants a word with you two. He can't believe how stupid you are. You think you are the only ones who can go back and forth to the future and have a tale to tell in the present?"

28

A Brindisi for All Time

Shackled hands and feet, in an upright position against the wall of what I assumed was Bnindagun's private and secret dungeon for Waywards, Brex and I stood side by side, anxiously counting the seconds and wondering what time would soon bring our way.

Time. Such a flexible, elastic concept, yet rigid also in its own way.

Certainly, human perception of it is highly variable. A moment of pain or grief can seem to last forever, while a happy time passes without a thought. A ten-year-old feels on December 1 as if Christmas will never come, but that same person will on his death bed at age 83 look back and feel his entire life has vanished in hardly more than a moment.

Finally there was a heavy knock at the door—by the sound of it, made by that ghastly doorknocker I had noted on the way in, a bronze figure of ol' Beelzebub himself. Surely the general had placed it there on purpose to set the tone, to unnerve his victims before even applying the first of his many tools on their tender flesh. I caught glimpses of some of his beastly tools along the walls, but tried not to look.

As the guard on the inside of the door opened it, I glanced at Brex, cool as a margarita in a blender. I couldn't tell if he knew something I didn't, had a plan already on how to get us out, or had somehow just psyched himself into his happy place so as to show no fear.

In walked Alain and a very attractive youngish man who looked awfully familiar. He practically glowed with light, reminding me of Lucifer, who always appeared not as a slimy, dragon-like fiend, as portrayed in much medieval art, but as an angel of light, that is, a fallen angel, but one retaining much of his original luster when appearing before mere humans.

As the man-devil eyed us, Brex rattled his chains. "You are the high priest of Enki who wanted to sacrifice all of us on that ziggurat in Ubaidian Mesopotamia."

I recognized him now. Whereas then he was dressed in flowing priestly garments, now he was dressed as any other modern UN delegate in a fine tailored suit. But the same cruel, inhuman light shone in his eyes like before.

"Yes, Mr. Herndon—or should I say, Dr. Brains?"

That almost made me snicker, despite the dire circumstances.

He gave me an offhand glance, but then focused on Brex. "I've been with General Bnindagun since the beginning."

I cleared my throat. "The beginning of what? This plot to conquer and master the world?"

"The beginning of recorded human time. The beginning, thousands of years ago as you understand it, when humanity was as one, and we all spoke the same language, and all had the one goal of a unified world with a grand central tower that would allow us to reach into the heavens and become like the gods."

"Only *He* wrecked your plans," said Brex, arching his head back and raising his eyes up towards the heavens on the word.

I glared at Brindisi. "He confounded your language, split your unity, and spread you in diverse directions across the face of the whole earth."

Brex looked nervous. "And ever since then, you two have led the way to restoring a false global unity... with you two ruling over it all."

"False? I think not. It's all quite real."

"No, it's not," said Brex. "It is a counterfeit. You force people to conform to your vision or die. Anyone who disagrees with you must be eliminated. The only real unity is among the elite leaders such as you two and your closest confederates, the true believers who have determined to rule the rest of humanity with absolute power."

"Better to rule in Hell than serve in Heaven, as Milton put it."

I remembered reading *Paradise Lost* in high school. Part of it, anyway. "You've certainly lost your shot at Paradise, Brindisi."

Brexxie's eyes narrowed. "So, you two somehow found or developed a method for travel back and forth in time? Or have you been here all along, all the hundreds of generations, using the device to keep alive in each and every time?"

Brindisi smiled, and I could imagine that mouth trying to devour human souls in a goblet, tossing them to the back of his throat again and again to achieve a satisfaction he would never know.

"A bit of both, actually. Einstein explained it best in his theory of relativity. A traveler hypothetically leaving earth at the speed of light could return just a few days later in his time, as he experienced it, only to find that a hundred years had passed on earth and all his family and friends who stayed behind were long dead."

Brexxie's eyes flashed in one of those *aha* moments. "So from the point of view of humans living a normal lifespan on earth, you keep appearing as young and vigorous and healthy from one generation to the next."

"I knew you'd understand."

"But why play time hopscotch and drop in on one generation after another?"

Brindisi walked along the wall towards us, lovingly stroking his many hideous implements with his left hand. "I needed the time and the experience to accumulate vast wealth beyond the wildest imagination of any mortal living a single life, or even of a multi-generational family dynasty."

"So you use your knowledge of the future to make money in incredible amounts here and there, use various means to store it for another generation, then drop back in and multiply it further?"

"Precisely. It is gratifying to at last find someone of my own intellectual caliber who can appreciate the magnitude of what I and the general have achieved." He paused beside a particularly ugly tool with multiple sharp barbs and gently lifted it from its wall latch, enjoying its heft and balance in his hand.

Brexxie's eyes widened at the sight "So if I run down a list of the wealthiest men in all of recorded history, I won't see your name perhaps, but you will have been there, maybe in the foreground, maybe behind the scenes, but constantly taking your cut and expanding your own fortune?"

"Try me, and we'll see."

"King Midas!" I interrupted.

"I was there. That business about turning things into gold with a mere touch is of course a myth. But with my help, he and his wife Damodice became the first rulers in world history to mint coins. That and his trade with Greece ensured his wealth. And as one of his principal advisors, I made sure I knew where the richest treasures were buried."

"Too obvious," said Brex. "I want to go sequentially. William the Conqueror, by some estimates the wealthiest man of the entire eleventh century."

"I was there. I'm the one who advised him to postpone his invasion of England until the English under King Harold had nearly exhausted their forces repelling the Viking invasion by King Hardrada just weeks earlier in that same year, 1066."

"Genghis Khan in the twelfth century."

Brindisi replaced the barbed tool and patted another one with a rounded lever that looked quite innocent, but surely wasn't. "He fought and conquered an empire of four billion acres, but I'm the one who taught him how to plunder it and accumulate the wealth in central locations."

"Filippo di Amedeo de Peruzzi in the thirteenth century."

Brindisi stepped away from the tools and walked softly towards me, staring as if to estimate what he needed to handle me. "He had already become wealthy with a shipping empire, but I was the one who helped him employ that capital to build the world's first family banking dynasty."

"Mansa Musa I in the fourteenth century."

"No. I stayed out of that one. He basically just lucked out by being king of the Malian Empire in West Africa, a land that just happened to be extraordinarily rich with minerals like gold and other natural resources."

"Jakob Fugger in the fifteenth century."

I matched Brindisi's stare, and he clucked and walked away. "Certainly. He made a fortune in shipping, but I helped teach him how to use his wealth to buy political influence and real power. A billionaire needs to have politicians in his pocket who can be counted upon to help him preserve and expand his wealth."

I could hardly believe all the things I was hearing. "So that's why so many pols today, even those who rail against the one percent and Wall Street, in actuality get millions in campaign cash and then turn right around and support the very ones they said they despised?"

Brindisi laughed, pointed at me, and asked Brex, "Is he really that naïve?"

"No," said Brex. "He's just overwhelmed at hearing of a side of history he knew next to nothing about. So you were the one who got Fugger to financially support Charles the Fifth's campaign to become emperor of the Holy Roman Empire?"

Brindisi paused next to Brex, but eyed him more cautiously, as if perceiving him as more of a threat. "Not directly. But I knew in whose ear to whisper the things that Charles needed to hear. And it paid off handsomely. As emperor, Charles gave Fugger the right to mint his own money, and that's where I came in. I helped set up the entire minting and distribution system... making certain I got a huge cut, of course."

"Sixteenth century."

"Oh, even I know that one," I interrupted. "The Ottoman Empire. Some sultan or other."

"Suleiman the Magnificent," said Brindisi, sparing me a short glance. "I stayed clear of him personally, but played a role in various regions of his far-flung empire."

"I would have avoided him, too," said Brex. "Too much court intrigue, along with insurrections, rebellions, and brutal crackdowns. Suleiman even had some of his own sons and grandsons murdered when he caught them plotting against him."

"Exactly," said Brindisi, peering at the clock on the wall as if expecting someone. "I've generally stayed out of the forefront and like to linger in the background with little to no attention on me. That's why you'll see nothing in the history books about my dealings in the seventeenth century with Aurangzeb, with Stephen Girard in the eighteenth, nor with the American robber barons or Middle Eastern oil potentates more recently."

"Practically no one today has even heard of you," said Brex, "yet you control the political fortunes of most nations on earth and nearly all the communication media and global trends."

"Time for you to shut up, Dr. Brains—and you, too, Mr. Brawn—and for us to get down to business. I know you were stalling for time while getting information on my background and plans. I didn't mind, because I needed time also for my minions to set up something very delightful for you two."

My heart thumped audibly.

He ran a caressing eye over his wall of hideous toys, a satisfied smile touching his lips. "You challenged Bnindagun to a duel eight thousand years ago, Dr. Herndon, and I am hereby challenging you to a second duel now."

Am I going to have to fight some rogue giant again?

"I know what you must be thinking, Mr. Brawn. But this will be the opposite of the first. You will play no role." Turning to Brex he said, "I challenge you, Dr. Herndon, to a duel. Mano a mano."

"You want to fight me?"

"Not physically, of course. But intellectually. You are the smartest man of his own generation ever in world history. I never achieved as much as you in any one generation, but I have lived through four hundred generations and have accumulated eight thousand years worth of wisdom and experience firsthand."

"So what happens if I win?"

"You and your friend get to live, walk out of here, and return to your life as you knew it before encountering me. Your superiors ordered you not to interfere with me to begin with, but you persisted. If you drop that here and now and go back to the tasks you are allowed to work on, then we can wash our hands of each other and go our separate ways."

"Never!" I spat out. "I would rather die first."

"That can easily be arranged." He waved his arm in an arc, sweeping along the walls of the room, where his nefarious instruments of pain and death were arrayed on hooks. "I might even let you choose the tool I'll use."

"What if I lose?" asked Brex.

"If you play me fair and square, and still lose, I'll make it quick, at least. Alain will dispatch you with bullets to the head. You won't really feel a thing. But you must promise to play me to the best of your abilities. I must know whether or not I am the smartest human of all time."

"What is our contest?"

"One that I know you are familiar with. Zantu four-dimensional chess."

"With sixteen players, each on a platform eight squares long, eight wide, eight levels in depth, and over eight time periods?"

"Yes."

"With standard one-minute times?"

"Certainly. I'll play fair and square by the standard rules, as will you, my worthy opponent. But there is one minor modification, just to keep it interesting."

Uh oh. The last time I heard that, I was in for a very unpleasant surprise.

"Standard game play rules, but instead of inanimate game pieces, we'll use live ones. That's why I needed a bit of time for my minions to set up the game board. Alain, if you will..."

Alain pressed a button, and the panel on our right, adorned with implements of butchery, slid out of sight. A thin plexiglass panel separated us from another room, now visible. It was quite large and held within it an enormous three-level game apparatus.

Along the bottom, two back rows of the right side, sitting bound in a chair with a gag in his mouth, was Jacques Bouchard, along with fifteen other bound figures I did not recognize.

Along the bottom, back two rows of the left side, were also sixteen bound figures, among them Linda, Momma Sara, Little Sara, Tara, and BigBear.

I strained against my shackles to no avail. It was hard to avoid screaming.

29

Zantu Four-Dimensional Chess

Brindisi noted our agony with a cross between a gloat and a grimace. "Don't worry. You can see them through the one-way mirror, but they can't see you. It wouldn't be fair to allow you to be distracted by them pleading out to you. They will only hear the moves as you and I call them out. And the pieces will move automatically as dictated. They'll catch on soon enough."

"You'd better not harm them," Brex said.

I knew how much harm I was prepared to dish out to Brindisi if I could get my hands on him...

"If you—or any of them—fail to cooperate or attempt to foil the game, Alain here need only press a button and a needle within the seat of whichever one he designates will eliminate that player. If the whole game goes awry, he can pull that lever and all the playing pieces will succumb to sarin gas."

I had to know something. "You know we are going to cooperate, but what happens when a playing piece is taken by one's opponent?"

"Isn't it obvious? That piece will no longer be living and will be removed from the board."

Brex and I looked at each other with the recognition that however he played this game, he couldn't afford to lose certain key players.

"But who are playing these other pieces? I don't recognize most of them."

"You don't need to know. Let's just say they are people who have crossed me one way or another, and I don't care what happens to them. Some have played this game before and survived to play again."

Some of these may just be goons who failed at their evil missions... some may be factions who tried to carve out more power for themselves or stole money from Mr. Big... but some may be patriots just like us who want to foil his plan of global conquest.

"You may now call the first move, Dr. Herndon."

"Do you mind if I use the pre-1980 notation system instead of the currently approved algebraic form? I think my friend here will be able to understand the flow of the game better that way. He is rather primitive and simple-minded, you see, at least as compared to us."

Brindisi nodded agreement. "He is rather strong, though."

"Yes," said Brexxie. "Quite *forceful*."

Brex put a heavy emphasis on that first syllable. *Force equals mass times acceleration. What is Brexxie trying to tell me?*

"State your first move, Mr. Herndon. I will wait no longer."

"Pawn to queen's bishop, level two, time two."

The poor schmuck in that position squirmed and looked panicky as his seat began to move forward, rise, and slowly head to his new position. I guessed he wouldn't arrive until the second time period.

Brindisi stroked his chin. "An interesting choice. You open with the first step of the classic but elementary Matterhorn maneuver. Either you think I am a poor player or you are trying to psych me out by making me think you are overconfident."

"There's one way to find out, Mr. Brindisi."

"Yes... Alain, if you please, queen's knight to level three, time one."

In a flash, that poor schlub was jolted into his new spot during this same time period. I wasn't counting seconds, but the first period should be over soon.

I was still trying to figure out Brexxie's message to me. To what could I apply force but the shackles at both wrists and both ankles? I decided to try slowly straining with all my might at each one in turn. But I couldn't move suddenly or make noise or call attention to myself. I looked up and all three of them controlling the game seemed focused entirely on it.

Brexxie's head turned back and forth as he calculated the subsequent follow-ons to each possible move. "Queen's bishop to level three, time two—"

Alain interrupted. "Time two begins now!"

Brex continued. "—take knight."

BigBear, all bound and muffled and sagging limply in his chair as if sedated, suddenly was propelled into the position the knight was holding. That unfortunate fellow flinched as the needle from his seat shot poison into his thigh, and by the time his seat had dumped him into the playing piece bin, he appeared dead.

Everyone was focused on him, so I gradually applied all the force I had to my left ankle shackle. Lord only knew how long the dungeon had been there and how many had struggled against those bonds, but the cumulative effect and my force now did make that ankle chain seem a bit loose.

Brindisi stroked his chin. "Masterful and adroit change of strategy at just the right moment of transition, Mr. Herndon. So you were psyching me out. I'll not underestimate you again. Are you sure you won't reconsider and join me? I would immediately free all your people and together you and I could rule the world."

"You are so terribly kind, Mr. Brindisi, but I have no interest in ruling the world. My goal in life is to help preserve a free world. Your move."

"Alain, if you will, queen to queen knight's pawn, level four, time three."

As that helpless character began to move towards his new spot, I tried the right ankle. No dice; that one seemed secure.

Brexxie hauled in a deep breath. "Queen's pawn to level four, time three."

I couldn't believe it. For the first time, one of our family was now exposed. Linda, his intended after only one date and one kiss, was apparently the queen, and the pawn in front of her was moving away. She looked scared.

I struggled with my right wrist, as inconspicuously as possible. Seemed to be a lot of play there, making me wonder what paroxysms of agony had led previous occupants to strain helplessly against these chains bolted to the wall behind them.

Brex's veneer of cool was gone now. As I had suspected, it had been all bravado from the start, a kind of self-hypnosis to keep his mind clear from stress so he could think. But now that he had exposed his own beloved in the game, the stress was winning. His usually relaxed expression now displayed furrowed brows, pinched lips, and pale cheeks. Hadn't he once told me something about controlling emotions? It was no longer working.

It was up to me now. I tugged with my left wrist.

Brindisi crowed triumphantly. "Queen's knight pawn to level four, time three. Take pawn."

Alain raised his right arm. "Time three starts in three, two, one," and Brindisi's pawn took Brexxie's.

As before, a needle shot into the thigh of that playing piece, and he appeared to be unconscious or dead by the time his seat tipped him over into the playing piece bin. In his case, however, his gag slipped and he screamed in horror as his final moments unfolded.

It was a shriek I'll never forget. I knew my two Saras had to be terrified, but I didn't look. I used the sound to mask what I was doing, pulling my left wrist chain completely free of the wall with a rapidly accelerating final jerk.

To mask my next task—using both hands to pull the right wrist chain from the wall—I shouted as loudly as I could, "I can't take this any more, Brexxie! Accelerate! *Accelerate!*"

He glanced at me, noted my progress, then shouted, "Queen to level three, time three, take pawn."

Poor Linda looked scared as her seat began to propel her forward and up to nearly the other side of the board on level three, but then a strange calm seemed to envelope her as she faced the pawn in front of her and watched him die. It was Jacques Bouchard, and she did not seem in the slightest upset by his passing.

I noticed only briefly, because I was on the floor, pulling my left ankle chain free, then immediately focusing on the right ankle chain with all the strength in my entire body. The surrounding concrete began to crumble.

I didn't see, but from what I could hear, BigBear must have awakened, gotten loose, and hopped off his seat, and now was running around the board barking. Just the distraction I needed.

With alarm in his voice, Brindisi yelled out, "Alain, kill the dog!"

Before they realized I was free, I stood up, chains dangling from both wrists and dragging from both ankles. The rattling alerted them to the danger as I charged over there as fast as possible, simultaneously wrapping up the wrist chains in my fists. I wrapped one chain around Alain's neck like a garotte and pulled him back from the control board before he could press any more buttons or levers.

In panic, Brindisi burst open the door and began to call out to the guards just outside. I kicked an ankle chain after him, tripping his feet, and he plunged into both guards as they responded.

Their stumbling gave me the two seconds I needed to snap Alain's neck, punch the shackle release button of the control board to free Brexxie, and hit the raise window lever to give him access to our loved ones. Then I ripped out the control panel with brute force, so that no one could use it to release the poison gas.

As the two remaining guards plunged at me, I crashed the control panel into their skulls, and they crumpled at my feet.

Brindisi struggled to his feet and raced in the direction of the time train. "This isn't over, Breslin Herndon! We'll finish this game another time in another place!"

I didn't try to stop him. He would propel himself to some other time, live another generation or two, and attempt to gain the whole world while losing his own soul. More people would die through his plots and schemes, but this point in time was secure. We could afford to let him run, for now.

I had no doubt we would encounter him again, but right now, in this place and this time, we had to free our loved ones.

Tears welled up in my eyes as I freed my two Saras, who clung to me as if to life itself, while BigBear kept leaping up and trying to join the hug circle.

30

Linda

When I could see again, I noted Brexxie had freed Linda and was hugging her and kissing her... fully on the lips this time. Of the two, he seemed the more emotional.

"Brexxie, you sure know how to show a girl a good time."

"Sorry, baby."

"You know, I kind of like this game. I would like to play it again some time."

"Whatever you want, sweet'ums."

"But without the death part, of course. Just the game itself, I mean."

"*Ja, natürlich.*"

"*Ah, mein Liebling.*" And she kissed him again, cradling his cheeks in her hands.

"*Willst du mich heiraten?*" he asked.

"*Ja. Ja! Sicherlich ja!*"

"What did he say?" I asked Sara.

"It's German. I think they just got engaged!"

"You're kidding! At a time like this? I'm still shaking."

I really was, but if Brex and Linda could both be that cool after what we had just been through, they certainly were a matched pair. I wanted to pretend to be cool myself. I walked over and patted Brexxie on the back.

He seemed to be floating. "You, you can be my best man, dear Jacks, yes, yessiree you can."

Linda turned to Sara. "I don't have any sisters. Would you be my matron of honor?"

Sara still looked shaken as well, but somehow stammered out, "I... I'd be honored!"

"May I be your flower girl, Auntie Linda?" asked Little Sara.

"Of course, sweetheart."

"And can Auntie Tara be a bridesmaid, too?"

Hearing that, Tara, still visibly quivering and with tears in her eyes, walked over and hugged her twin and Little Sara.

"Of course, angel. Tara, would you do me the honor?"

At first she couldn't speak, but she nodded. Then she struggled to find her tongue. "Absolutely! If... if you're going to join this crazy family, we should get to know each other as well as possible."

I turned serious for a moment, waving my hand at the still bound and seated players we didn't know. "Brex, what about them? Should we let the authorities sort this out?"

"Territorial sovereignty, remember? And I don't trust the UN people to sort out their own mess. There are lots and lots of good, honest people working here, but also too many foxes to trust them to hunt down the other foxes. I think we have to just let them all go right now without worrying which is good, bad, or ugly, and just hope for the best. Many if not most are patriots who stood in Brindisi's way. And even the ones formerly from his team hate his guts now, and the enemy of my enemy is my friend."

Linda hugged Brex around the waist. "How are you feeling, sweet thing?"

He grinned at her. "Kinda weak, actually. I think I just burned up the last of my cerebral glucose plotting out those four-dimensional chess moves."

"Baby, I've got just the right thing for you," and she pulled a bright yellow pack of Peanut M&Ms from a pocket in her jacket. "Sara filled me in on the whole story, and I want to always be there for you."

Brex beamed, gave her a quick kiss on the lips, then popped an oval of chocolate relief into his mouth. He winked at me. "This is a match made in heaven!"

31

Loose Ends

Brex and I waited patiently in the CIG HQ parking lot at Fort Meade, Maryland, right near the old NSA building. We kept out of sight behind Brexxie's Honda Odyssey SUV rental, and every now and then, getting more fidgety by the minute, I used the side mirrors to glance at Addams' parked silver Mercedes.

Assistant CIG Director Addams was a man of habit, as Brex had noted in his secret lab while reviewing tapes of his movements over the past few days, and I noted from a distance now that he was right on time as he exited the building and headed our way.

As soon as he unlocked his car and started sliding into his seat, I signaled Brex and darted over to the driver's window, my .45 drawn and cocked with the safety off. He saw me, and I signaled for him to lower the window.

He did. "You'll never get away with it. You know you're on tape right now. There's cameras all over the place."

"Get away with what?"

He nodded toward the gun.

"Oh, that. That's just to get your attention. We only want to talk. Let us in."

He sighed but unlocked the door.

Brex and I both got in the back. "You're the one who'll never get away with it," I said.

"With what?"

"We know you're the one who tipped off Brindisi that we were getting too close to his time travel scheme to overwhelm America with barbarians from the distant past."

"You were ordered to stand down and not pursue this line of investigation. If you had just obeyed orders, none of this would have happened."

Brex scowled. "I have news for you, Mr. Director. Real Americans don't obey unconstitutional orders. We're not little socialist, globalist toadies like you!"

"So now what? Are you going to kill me?"

"No," I said. "We aren't going to lay a finger on you. We're going to give you a chance to do the right thing."

"The right thing? The right thing?" He let go of the steering wheel and tugged on his hair helplessly with his left hand. "I don't even know what the right thing is any more!"

"That's only because you let yourself be seduced by the Dark Side of the globalist Force. If you start thinking like a real American again, it will come back to you."

"*Seduced?* You think it was that easy? That I just succumbed out of a lust for riches or power? I was scared out of my wits by Brindisi's threats and did what I had to do to survive. And if you had any sense at all, you'd do the same."

"There's always been evil in this world, and there always will be. But that doesn't mean we shouldn't fight it!" I said.

"I'm going to lay it out for you as simply as I can. There are dark forces in this world which control nearly everything and pull nearly all the strings of power. You can't touch them. You need to lower your sights and attack the little pockets of bad here and there. Brindisi and his bunch will allow people like you to nick here and there at the little hangnails of their tentacles of power."

I hooted. "Allow? We don't ask permission from some world-conquering tyrant."

"Well, you should. Just play sheriff and bad guys on a low level and you'll be fine. They'll let you take down a drug dealer here or there, or a con man or terrorist or maybe a sex trafficking pervert... you know, the kinds of things in the news which lull the masses into thinking that law enforcement is making real progress. But only so long as the real bigwigs behind it all skate scot-free. If you threaten any central artery of his power or go after the creature himself or his main co-conspirators, he'll unleash the hounds of Hell on you."

Brex leaned forward and spoke in a low but firm voice. "We're not going to sit here and argue with you any more. You have three choices: One, we can spend as long as it takes, up to the rest of our lives, gathering the evidence of your malfeasance and take it to the National Security Council. Or, two, you can turn yourself in and confess right now. Maybe turn state's evidence if you have the guts to go into the Witness Protection Program. Or, three—"

I pushed it toward him. "—here's your .38 Special revolver from your nightstand at home. Loaded with your usual +P shells. Personally, I would prefer a .357 Magnum, but when the police investigate, they'll expect +P from you."

He made a kind of gurgling, gargling sound deep in his throat, and his eyes flew open wide. But he refused to take the revolver.

I wiped my fingerprints off with a white handkerchief and set the pistol on the front seat beside him. "Do the right thing now, Addams. This... or confess... or game on. Entirely up to you."

Without another word, we left the car, softly closing the doors so as not to interrupt his line of thought. Before we had traversed the ten yards back to our Odyssey, a gunshot coughed, muffled by the doors and windows of a car.

We didn't look back. There was no triumph, no joy, in removing a traitor who had once been a loyal member of the team.

I leaned toward Brex. "I suppose Internal Affairs will take one look at those digital recordings and we'll spend the next couple of days being interrogated about all this."

"Nah, I don't think so," said Brex. "I think they're going to be stunned and befuddled, though, when they find the recordings from all the cameras focused on this spot, by amazing coincidence, all failed for precisely the period that you and I were out here."

A knot in the pit of my stomach relaxed. "Ah, nice one, Brexxie. Very nice."

I was watching the news on the telly back home and couldn't believe what I saw. I signaled Brexxie on the intercom and asked him if he were too busy or could he join me to see an astonishing story.

His voice was crisp. "Well, I'm not doing much important. Just working on a way to save the world from its next big crisis. We defeated Bnindagun in our past and future, but he's still here in our present. He's still running mobs of barbarians throughout the country. Tackling him and his goons in the here and now is our next mission."

"That's cool with me, but at this particular moment I'm concerned with something else."

"Oh, in that case, I'll put saving civilization on the back burner and come toast marshmallows on the campfire with you."

"Ha, ha. Very funny, Brex. I want to know right now if these are some marshmallows you already toasted."

"Coming, good buddy." In a flash he stood beside me.

"Brex, I just saw an amazing story about the UN and I need to know if you are behind it."

"You don't need to know diddly. The less you know about anything, the better. That way, if any of our bosses decide to cross-examine you all night, you can honestly say you know nothing. That's likely what they expect from you anyway, to know nothing."

"You're a regular stand-up comic tonight, Brex."

"So what do you want to know?"

"There's the strangest report on all the network news shows. Something about an explosive of some kind in the sewer system under the UN complex. But I don't suppose you know anything about that?"

"Explosive, you say? Well, animal and human waste does produce a lot of methane, a carbon-based gas which is highly explosive if compressed enough and ignited."

"I'm not laughing, Brex. This isn't *Comedy Central Presents*."

"Well, even you know methane is explosive, right? Maybe there was a build-up of methane gas and someone near a leaking pipe was smoking a cigar and set it off. I've heard of manhole covers in the open street exploding ten feet in the air from that sometimes."

"Very interesting, Brex," said I. "But I was thinking it could have also been caused by a particularly smart and clever person guiding a torpedo of some kind through the sewer system to just the right spot and then detonating it."

"An interesting thought, but perhaps you've seen too many of those *Mission Impossible* movies."

"I don't think so."

"So anyway, what happened to the UN?"

"The whole site will be unusable for at least six months."

"What a shame. So what will all the delegates do?"

"The prime minister of Canada has offered to let them use the Parliament buildings in Ottawa until repairs can be completed."

"How nice! Six months, you say?"

"Yeah, but you know it will be a union job. Whenever a union is involved, it's liable to take longer than first predicted."

"Well, how sad! What a shame the UN won't be occupying space in New York City or anywhere in the United States for a while. What a loss. Whatever shall we do?"

I snickered. "I, for one, will be crying into my beer every night."

"You don't suppose those union guys, when they get in there to do their work, will maybe find the remains of a hidden dungeon or a secret time train station or something?"

"Nope... the basement of that building is the very spot that was totally destroyed. Yet the thirty-nine stories above sustained almost no damage at all. It's almost as if the methane cloud somehow intentionally went to that very spot, and knew just when to explode so that no one was in the building or got hurt. But you wouldn't know anything about that, would you?"

"Oh, I know lots about methane, its combustibility, and all its combustion by-products. If our superiors decide to investigate, I could testify literally all day and all night about its chemical formula, CH_4, the amount of energy produced by each gram of gas, the explosive impact, the comparability to TNT or even nukes—in terms of blast intensity and radius, I mean—the—"

"Thank you, Brex, that will be all."

"You're dismissing me like a servant?"

"Not a servant. You are the master of all. A grandmaster of Zantu four-dimensional chess. You are in a class all by yourself. You are an astonishment for the ages."

"Why, thank you, my dear Jacks."

"Man, but I'm glad you're on our side."

"So am I, dear Jacks, so am I."

32

Home Again

Brex and Linda were out on the town again, or perhaps making out at her place. I couldn't be sure, for he had become quite secretive about how quickly their relationship was progressing.

Momma Sara and I planned to go to the Spyscape museum downtown and check out the new exhibits. It was a Friday evening, and they had a special James Bond theme dinner, complete with martinis shaken not stirred. It sounded like fun, and who knew—I might even learn something from all the exhibits on famous cases of real spying over the decades.

Tara had agreed to come babysit Little Sara for the evening, and a few minutes later I saw my sister-in-law standing at the kitchen sink washing a couple of apples. I crept up behind her and slipped my arms around her waist. I nuzzled the back of her neck and whispered, "Let's forget the museum tonight, baby. Let Tara take Little Sara instead, while you and I stay here and have a different kind of fun."

I could feel her stiffen, and she whispered back, "You know it's me, right?"

"Oh, yeah, baby. My wife, mother of my child."

She stamped her right foot, turned off the water, twisted out of my grasp, and pulled a couple of feet away, glaring at me.

Just then Momma Sara entered the room. "What's going on here?" she demanded, hands on her hips.

I glanced back over my shoulder, but only briefly. "Not now, Tara. I'm about to make love to my wife. Take Little Sara and the dog for a walk or something."

"Jack Rigalto!" both of them yelled simultaneously.

I couldn't control myself any longer and burst out laughing. "Wait, now who is who? You both look so much alike!"

"Okay, wisenheimer." Tara put the wet apples on a paper towel beside the sink. "I'm Tara and you know it."

"No!" I exclaimed, tongue in cheek. "Tara's the one by the door!"

Sara started giggling now. "My dear Jacks, we're going to have to get Brexxie to spend more time with you like in the old days. You're getting coocoo with your best friend gone all the time."

"We're *not* best friends, Sara. Just good buddies."

"Right. And Tara's not my twin. She's just a sister."

Tara giggled. "Don't worry, Jack. Once they get married, he'll settle down again. You certainly did."

"Thanks, Tara. By the way, did Linda tell you she has a brother coming in from out of town for the wedding who wants to meet you? He teaches physical therapy at the University of Chicago."

She looked flustered and began to speak at twice her normal speed. "You mean *the* famous Dr. Richard Cesnick, one of the most important figures in our field, is Linda's brother?"

"Yes! I spoke to him on the phone this morning before Brex and Linda left. I told him about you and your new book. He's very interested and eager to meet you. And he is single, in case you are wondering."

"Single? Meet *me*? Thanks, brother-in-law!" She bounded over and gave me a peck on the cheek and then a quick hug. She bubbled like freshly poured champagne. "Oh, my gosh! When is he getting here? What am I going to wear? Sara, you've got to go shopping with me tomorrow in Manhattan so I can get something appropriate. Maybe Saks Fifth Avenue or Bloomingdale's."

Sara beamed. "Of course! I'm also partial to Bergdorf Goodman or Neiman Marcus, if you can't find what you want at the first two."

"That's a great idea," I said. "I'll take a day off and stay with Little Sara and BigBear and you two can do your sister thing in Manhattan. And lunch is on me—wherever you like. Sounds like fun."

"Thanks, Jack. Thank you, thank you, thank you."

"Well, Tara, it's the least I can do after all the times you've dropped everything on your plate to come babysit our daughter. So, thank you for all those many times. It would have been tough without you."

Tara was beaming and practically floating in the air.

Sara gave me a wink and a warm smile.

"Make sure you pick a time when Bill Higgins can make it. It wouldn't be the same without him."

"You got it, buddy," I said.

Brexxie and I were making plans for his bachelor party when the doorbell rang.

In a moment Momma Sara stuck her head through the doorway. "Package for you guys. Special delivery. It's too big and heavy for me to carry."

Big? Heavy? My first thought was a bomb. I hurried to the front door.

It was from the White House.

"What do you think it is this time?" wondered Brexxie out loud.

"Let's find out." I whipped out my Smith and Wesson folding knife and set to work. Several bottles of something new to me, each carefully wrapped in paper, had been inserted in a cardboard cube within the larger box. I pulled one out and showed it to Brex and Sara.

"Antarctic Nail Ale!" Brex beamed as he took the bottle from me and admired it. "I've read about this. The Australians brew using water obtained by melting chunks of a real Antarctic iceberg. This is even rarer and more expensive than that Sam Adams Utopia he sent before. I believe this one costs about $800 a bottle."

Sara beamed. "Well, it's nice that someone appreciates the work you guys do."

Just then Little Sara and BigBear ran in to see what the excitement was all about. "More beer?" she lamented. "Don't ask me to sniff it again. Beer is so *yuck!*"

At last the house was empty, except for BigBear, who was napping near a warm HVAC vent.

I found Sara in the kitchen finishing the dishes. She turned to me with that cute quizzical look, and I hugged her tight. I kissed her passionately and hard on the lips, then did what I called my dancing kiss, where I cradled her cheeks in my palms, pressed my entire body tightly against hers and could feel and almost hear her heartbeat, tilted her face up to meet mine as I bent down, then nuzzled the right side of her neck, kissed her right cheek, then nose and left cheek, then blew a warm and humid, sultry breath into her left ear. I could always feel the sexual electricity zinging through her system and exploding up her spine at that point.

She was limp putty in my arms and ready for any dance move I might suggest, either upright with music on, or prone in bed... or on the sofa... or maybe the kitchen table or the carpet in front of the fireplace.

I loved those kisses.

But this time, as she clung to me expectantly, caught in that delicate balance between inchoate desire and breathless anticipation, she hesitated. She eased back from the waist up, but without removing her feet from between mine. "Are we ever going to have a normal life? Or will it always be fighting for our lives?"

"No one ever has a normal life," I said. "Life is what happens when all your plans go awry and you just have to cope with whatever is left. The important thing is to have faith that there is a meaning and purpose behind it all and to go through it with someone you love and who loves you."

"Well, I love you," she whispered, and snuggled tight again.

I kissed her again. "And I love you."

"No one could thrill me like you, the man of my dreams, the man of my life, the man of my heart. But I have to admit you bring out a little bit of the cavegirl in me."

"Well, you certainly bring out the Neanderthal in me," I whispered.

"Then, baby, grab me by the hair and claim your reward."

"Oom-gawa,"

She giggled. "That's not Neanderthal. That's Tarzan."

"Oom-gawa. You Jane. Me Tarzan."

She giggled and mock-resisted as I lifted her up, tossed her over my shoulder, and stomped into the bedroom like a gorilla, throwing her gently on top of the bed.

I paused there quietly and took one long look at her, admiring every feature of her lovely face and womanly form, before joining her on the bed.

I took my time, slowly and gently savoring every moment.

As did she.

I could hear the chimps chattering in the trees above us as we made love...

END

ABOUT THE AUTHOR

Charles A. Salter has been a writer all his life. A professional member of the American Society of Journalists and Authors, he has published about two dozen books and hundreds of articles in magazines and newspapers, as well as numerous U.S. Government technical reports. His adult mystery novels and juvenile non-fiction books have earned excellent reviews and won various awards. Currently retired, he served for 28 years as a Medical Service Corps officer in the United States Army.

HAVE YOU READ.?.

If you liked this book, the first full-length Brex and Jacks (alias Brains and Brawn) novel, be sure to check out their first appearance in the short story "The Herndon Secret" in this short story anthology.

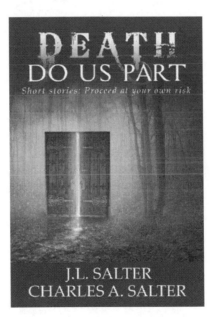

I had four hours to get my beloved Sara back... or they would kill her. And it wouldn't be anything so gentle as a fentanyl overdose.

And only Brexxie Herndon could help me now. I stared at him on the far side of my living room, leaning against the wall, shaking slightly and trying to catch his breath. The carpet between us and the sofa were covered in blood oozing from two dead bodies.

Brexxie—short for Breslin. Working for DARPA—the Defense Advanced Research Projects Agency. Said to be smarter than Einstein himself, but now on the lam. Everyone wanted the products sprouted from his intricate grey matter. Everyone: good, bad, or ugly.

"Why did you have to get me and Sara involved, Brexxie? I'm not active any more. You know I'm retired. I have no connections or pull at the Agency any longer."

"Sorry, Jacks. Really, dude. I never thought they'd take Sara."

"That's always your prob, Brex. You live in your own ivory tower. You can't seem to deal with the real world."

"Dealing with it now, dude. Big time. We both are."

"Yeah, all three of us are. If we can't find them soon and free her, Sara is a goner."

"I said I'm sorry, man! When I recognized they were following me, I couldn't think of anywhere else to turn. You were the only one at the Agency who ever treated me like a normal *Homo sapiens.*

I looked at his pale and pasty face, his not quite five-foot height, his almost emaciated frame—from too many office lunches of Peanut M&Ms instead of real food. I knew he had no chance against those thugs on his own, while I, despite being retired, was at least still strong and heavily armed—as the first punk who'd tried to grab Sara had soon learned, a .45 slug between his eyes and his inert grey matter splattering out the back of his head.

"So what secret weapon did you cook up this time, Brexxie? What were they after?"

Brexxie started to tremble. He opened his mouth to speak, but nothing came out. I stepped over the lifeless bodies of Punk #1 and #2—the second with a 12-inch Buck General knife in his chest—and grabbed Brex before he could collapse. The slightest stress nearly always gave him the shakes, or the faints, or the stumbles. He had chosen the wrong line of work after graduating top of his class from MIT... at the age of 16. He should have gone into civilian electronics work and made billions in the private sector world of computers, NOT into Defense work developing new spy satellites, micro-communication gear, and weird personal protection devices for spies.

"No BS, Brex. I don't care if my security clearance expired. You are going to tell me everything, or you and I will die the same as Sara. You got that?"

"Okay, Jacks. Okay. Just let me sit on your sofa for a second and catch my breath."

"So what is it? We're running out of time."

"I call it the Herndon Device."

"Modest as always, Brexxie."

"Well, I invented it, so I can call it whatever I want."

"At least until DARPA puts it in its Top Secret catalogue as part of its new funding request submitted to Congress. By then it'll have a name like 'Personal Protection Device, Microscopic, Electronic, Non-lethal Weapon'."

"Close, but no Havana, *Nicotiana tabacum*. You remember how a hundred years ago, musicians recorded directly on blank vinyl records or even more primitive disks? I'm not talking about recording studios, fancy equipment, or mass production. Just a lone artist or group making a single record in the basement."

"Before my time, but I've seen it in old movies and stuff. A microphone picked up soundwaves from voices and/or instruments, then vibrated a stylus to make grooves in the wax or plastic disk, which spun on a turntable."

"And how did it play back?"

"I think the turntable would spin at the same fixed speed as when recording, and the phonographic needle would follow that same track, the vibrations producing sound waves to be amplified and emitted by a speaker."

"Right," concluded Brexxie. "And my new invention is capable of picking up vibrations stored at the atomic level by any kind of motion and then playing them back as sounds and images of the events which just occurred in that vicinity."

I was stunned. Even for Brexxie, this was a dramatic innovation. "You mean you can get playback of any recent event recorded by objects in this room? Walls, the floor, a glass window?"

"Yessiree, I can indeed."

"You could read off these walls what just happened here?"

"Well, atoms are always in motion, so it is unpredictable how long a 'recording' will last in a stationary object such as a wall. You might get only a millisecond or two's worth of data. But if an object is spinning at a set rate, such as a ceiling fan or a microwave turntable, it makes a longer-lasting change in the pattern of atoms. You can usually get a minute or two of recording before the signal fades."

"Show me," I said...

Thanks for reading! Dingbat Publishing strives to bring you quality entertainment that doesn't take itself too seriously. I mean honestly, with a name like that, our books have to be good or we're going to be laughed at. Or maybe both.

If you enjoyed this book, the best thing you can do is buy a million more copies and give them to all your friends... erm, leave a review on the readers' website of your preference. All authors love feedback and we take reviews from readers like you seriously.

Oh, and c'mon over to our website:
www.DingbatPublishing.ninja

Who knows what other books you'll find there?

Cheers,

Gunnar Grey,
publisher, author, and Chief Dingbat

δ

Made in the USA
Middletown, DE
21 February 2021

34144540R00117